Published by Dragon Brothers Books Ltd
www.dragonbrothersbooks.com
Text © 2021 James Russell.
ISBN: 978-0-473-57072-9
Cover image: George Karbus
Book design: Suzanne Denmead

SALTWATER SERIES

LINES

James Russell

*"No sympathy for the devil; keep that in mind.
Buy the ticket, take the ride."*

Hunter S. Thompson

Chapter 1

When Anto picks me up it's still dark. As usual, he bangs on my window and yells, making enough noise to wake the whole neighbourhood. I jump out of bed and pull back the curtains to make him stop and he's all mad eyes and teeth through the window.

"Here's Johnny," he hisses, then gives me the finger and lopes off up the lane into the darkness.

I'm surprised that I didn't hear the Jeep because I was already lying awake, turning everything over and over in my mind, wondering if he'd come and hoping like fuck he wouldn't. My head's pounding and my mouth is thick with a sour chemical tang. I pull on some clothes, swallow some Panadol and take a long drink from the bathroom tap.

I have to lean hard on the front door to open it because the lock is still all bent to shit. Outside, I see Anto's taillights a little way up the road. The glow picks out the squat black beetle of the jetski tethered behind on its trailer and it sends a trickle of apprehension through me.

It's freezing, and I zip my puffer jacket against the cold.

I spit viscous saliva onto the frozen grass, trying unsuccessfully to expel my nausea. I grab my wettie, hood, booties, and gloves from the shed and wrap them all in a towel. Last night, when I got home, drunk and high as a kite, I remember grabbing the surfboard Anto bought for me and walking out into the moonlight. I stood there silently in the lane, admiring it. It's a monster – a gun, nine foot six, built for waves of consequence. Last night I could picture myself riding them; now all I feel is crushing self-doubt. I put it under my arm and trudge up the lane, the frosty gravel crunching under my shoes.

Anto sits on the bonnet of the Jeep. He looks jittery, nervous, scanning up and down the street. There are no lights on in the houses, not a soul on the road; no one in their right mind is out of the bed at this hour. I'm jittery too – it's an occupational hazard by this point.

He smiles when he sees me coming.

"Morning, Sam. You bring the rhino chaser?" he asks, nodding at my board. "Cos it's on, you Aussie bastard." He grins like a lunatic. As I get close I get a decent look at him. He's wired, his eyes on stalks; obviously he's pulled an all-nighter.

"How do you know it's on?" I say. "It's pitch dark."

"I can fucking feel it," he hisses, thumping my shoulder. He reeks of booze.

We take off with Anto's trademark screech of rubber and tear through the streets, the trailer clanking and jouncing behind us.

"I fucking love this car," says Anto.

Driving around the villages of the rural west of Ireland in this rig makes us stick out like a sore thumb, but there it is. Anto doesn't give a fuck. Dumb culchie boggers, he calls the locals, or hedge-hopping muppets.

We both stare at Donnaghy's Pub as we pass it. It was less than six hours ago that we'd stumbled out of it onto the silent street, mightily off our faces. Bren had held high a licked finger and solemnly declared that the wind had turned offshore. We'd agreed to surf in the morning.

"That was some craic, last night," says Anto. He's boggling around in his seat, checking the rear-view mirror, then twisting to look behind us. He's manic. He winds up the Jeep out of Bundoran and onto the open road.

"Yeah," I agree. "Are you still high?"

"As a fucking kite." He grins. "Bren and me had a few nightcaps."

"Was that wise, Anto?" I ask.

"Sorry, Dad," he replies.

Fifteen minutes later we go past Mullaghmore Harbour and I peer out into the darkness. There's no one around. Our headlights illuminate the wash of foam in the harbour. It's banked up against the stone walls and gathered around the fishing boats like suds in a bathtub; the residue from the oceanic machine agitating out there in the darkness.

When we drive up onto the head road, Anto pulls over, shuts off the engine, and winds down his window. A rumble, an energy – like a distant train – bullies its way in, filling the space with more than just sound. Anto's eyes bulge at me.

"It's big, Sam," he says, grabbing my arm. "It's fucking big." He squirms and bounces, peering out into the darkness.

We sit and wait. Anto grows more animated, more hyper, but I retreat into my own head, apprehension gluing up my thoughts, my words. He starts talking about later – the Dublin drop – but I've tuned him out.

Finally, Anto can't take it any longer; he jumps out of the Jeep, runs to the edge of the rocks, and starts pointing at things I can't see.

A ribbon of grey materialises on the horizon behind us. Morning's on its way. I look at my phone, checking for messages, hoping for safety in numbers, someone to talk sense. When Anto returns to the Jeep he comes around to my side and I wind down the window.

"I'll have a Big Mac combo please," he says, hopping from one foot to the other. He pulls off his beanie and his woolly hair springs out like a Brillo pad, adding to the crazy. But he looks hard at me, suddenly serious, and leans in close.

"There's not a puff of wind out there," he says. "I reckon we paddle it."

I swallow.

"Fuck, Anto… I'm hungover as shit… this is… " I mumble, but tail off lamely. I know that nothing I say is going to make any difference. His mind is made up. He confirms it.

"You coming or what?"

He doesn't pronounce the 't' in words, does Anto. 'You coming or wha?' Usually I give him shit about it, mimic him, but not today.

"We waiting for the others?" I say.

Anto smiles.

"Nah. Bren isn't coming, that's for sure. He was puking his guts up when I left him."

"What about Mikey?"

Anto shrugs.

"Who knows? Maybe he'll catch up," he says.

Anto flings opens the back of the Jeep and starts rummaging for his wetsuit. I get out, cross the road and sit down on a rock. The air is filled with an electricity, a saltwater charge. The sound booms in the darkness, seems to come from every direction all at once.

Anto is suited up by the time dawn starts to illuminate the bay. He sits down beside me, but his legs hammer up and down like sewing machines.

Only the whitewater can be seen at first; broad lines confusedly disassembling themselves on the rocks further up the point. Kelp whips and thrashes. Then, fifteen minutes later, the surf begins to reveal itself through the growing light. Giant grey-green slabs rear out of the deep, darkening ominously as they stand up on the reef. More increments of light reveal the cavernous dark barrels, the walls defying gravity as they haul themselves erect down the line and launch themselves towards shore. They seem to fold over in slow motion, an optical illusion created by their sheer size, the way a building seems to crumple ponderously after its foundations are dynamited.

Anto hops from foot to foot. He pronounces it triple overhead, but just as he does a set looms that re-calibrates his estimate.

"Oh fuck, oh fuck," he says. "Sam. Look at that thing."

We stand and stare as a giant wave turns itself inside out on the reef. The crack and boom of it breaking is like distant thunder; it travels to a place deep inside my gut. The wave pounds its way down the reef, great puffs of spray exploding through its roof, and being vomited from its mouth.

"Did you see how fucking perfect that was?" shouts Anto. But all I saw was the awful maelstrom, the violence.

I go around to the back of the Jeep to pick up my wetsuit, and I see all twenty packages of cocaine heaped carelessly in the back, the popped black balloons still attached to them. I can't believe Anto has just left them there like that. I can even see the ragged hole he put in one of them, and it scares the shit out of me. How the fuck did I get here, I think to myself.

My suit's still wet from two days ago, and stiff with the cold. By the time I'm into it Anto has hauled out both surfboards and is furiously waxing his.

I try one last time.

"Let's take the ski, Anto."

"Fuck that," he replies, not looking up. "This is our day, Sam."

"I'm out of my league, mate," I try, but Anto's having none of it.

"Bullshit," he replies. "You're better than all of us."

He finally stops waxing and looks up at me.

"I'll go out there on my own, I swear I will. I don't fucking want to, but I will."

I don't say anything, but instead pick up the half-block of wax Anto has left on the ground and start to rub it over my board.

Anto dives at me and lands on my back like Gollum in *The Lord of the Rings*. "You little ripper," he mocks in his awful Aussie accent. "You little fucking beauty!"

As we make our way down onto the rocks, I feel like I'm going to spew. I don't know if it's the hangover or sheer terror. I forget all about the drugs, about the Dublin drop. There's only me and the furious ocean in front of me. I hope like fuck there's a crew around at the boat ramp launching skis. Before we locked the Jeep, I sent a text to Mikey but there was no reply.

In close, there's a kind of mini lagoon, and the surface of the sea is black gloss; not a puff of wind blows in any direction, which is some sort of miracle because normally it's blowing forty bastards out here. Overhead, it looks like the day will be illuminated no further. Clouds like haematomas have arrived to cover the sky. This fucking country, I think. You can go three weeks without seeing the sun. I conjure an image of the coast of Western Australia, the endless blue of the ocean and the sky, the light like crystal; hard and delicate. Here, it's fifty shades of fucking grey.

I know what's ahead. It's a long paddle which starts in calm water and finishes twenty minutes later in an environment so violent and frightening my first instinct is always to turn around and paddle straight back in again. This is my third time out here, but the first in waves like this. We plunge in and paddle hard because the water is so cold. It seeps in through the seams in my wetsuit, works its way into my booties and gloves. My board – the gun – feels unwieldy and alien, like a tool I don't yet know how to use.

Once we break out of the lagoon and into deep water we have to paddle through a line of thick foam, which is all that remains of the leviathans expending themselves on the outer reef. Our hair isn't even wet. Even here there's a ton of water moving, and the speed of the sweep is mad, pushing us further into the bay until we can get well off the rocks and out of the current. Broad-backed swells thirty metres wide pulse below me. I can feel their power as I go over them; they lift and push me shoreward for an age before passing beneath me, depositing me into the trough.

We're halfway out to the top of the point when the sun peeps above the horizon, finding space between the hills and the cloud. But there's no rose-coloured glow to the sunrise. Instead, the ocean surface turns silver, like the scales of an enormous fish, and the waves look like collapsing piles of scrap metal. They steam towards us like cruise liners; each an entity of its own, seemingly dispossessed of the sea, and charged with an awful, freakish power. The noise as they break down the line is incredible. We're far enough out that I begin to spot the boils in front of the waves; they pulse and gush at the surface like geysers, the signs of submarine rocks I don't want to think about. I can't tear my eyes away from the barrel as we paddle up and over each wave; a gaping black cave with a concrete mixer churning furiously at the rear.

Anto is paddling hard. He's thirty metres in front of me, and just as he reaches the crest of a wave, I see him stiffen, pivot his board towards the channel and start hauling arse. I hear him yelp.

Immediately I turn out to sea too, even though I can't yet see what's coming. Ten seconds later I top the wave he went over, and revealed in front of me is a looming set that comes from another realm entirely. The wall of the first wave of the set seems to stretch out across the entire bay. It's going to close out and take Anto and me with it. It's already begun feathering, and he's well ahead of me, flat to his board and paddling for all he's worth. Fear rips through me, spurring me on, and I put my head down and paddle at an angle, but I know that I'm lost and I'm going to end up getting it squarely on the head. I suck in great, gasping breaths in an attempt to super-saturate my lungs in preparation for the beating. Instead, I find myself even more breathless, more panicked.

It seems to take forever, paddling across that flat expanse. Somehow Anto makes it over the top of the wave, but it's standing up now, hauling its appalling mass skyward to form a wall like the side of a barn. Deep inside, the wave begins to fold itself over, but I don't look at it – I can't – and as it breaks there's a crack that seems to split the air; as loud as a high-powered rifle.

Terror dulls my senses. I don't know whether to stop or keep going, but I do the latter, and I get five more strokes in before I realise I'm going to make it; the rock shelf here is so distinct, the channel so deep, that the wave doesn't close out after all, but screams across the reef with a terrifying precision.

The next wave is even bigger, but Anto and I get over it with ease. When the last wave in the set surges beneath me, I crest the peak and immediately see him sitting up on his board, a crazy grin plastered across his face.

Adrenaline gushes through me, along with relief. I sit up on my board too, shaking like a leaf.

"This is the fucking life, wha?" he screams.

I feel the wave of nausea rise like a tide, and I begin to vomit. For some reason I hold out my hands, as though I have to catch it.

Chapter 2

THREE MONTHS EARLIER

Bali's a trip. But maybe it's because it's the first time I've ever been anywhere other than Australia.

On Instagram it's all golden sunsets and waterfalls and dreamy blue ocean, but the airport is a zoo, and the drive across Bali is a smog-filled nightmare through gridlocked streets and the illusion well and truly shatters. An old man on a moped tries to overtake us and my taxi driver squeezes him until he actually nudges his handlebars. He wobbles like crazy, careens across the road into oncoming traffic and nearly gets mown down by a truck. My driver carries on without a sideways glance, and I can't decide whether he's blissfully unaware or simply doesn't give a shit. By the time I reach Uluwatu, I'm frazzled.

It's the tail end of the season for swell, and there are only little waves out front, but as soon as I check in to my losmen I'm out there, washing off the trip. I catch a few little runners but it's soft and mushy and the rising tide is only making it worse.

I go back to the losmen and order a Bintang. The sun starts to go down and finally it starts to feel like the ads.

e picked the party losmen, because there's a big
ssie lads and their girlfriends in the lounge and
etting stuck in to the beers and cocktails and the girls
ghing like hyenas. I listen in and they're funny fuckers and
t talking to one of the boys when he comes to the bar for a
ound of tequilas. His eyes are sporting an alcoholic glaze. It's
their last night in Indo before they fly back to Sydney. For the
past week they've been at G-Land with only small waves, and he's
absolutely spewing because of course now that they're about to
leave, there's a decent swell on its way. He tells me that there are
fuck-all people staying at the camps there, given that it's so late in
the season.

I'm glad to meet him because I haven't done my homework –
other than the guy at my local surf shop telling me I should head
for Uluwatu. I dropped eight hundred bucks on a new board that
he said was perfect for Indonesian waves.

He asks where I'm from, but when I tell him he hasn't heard of
it. I say when you live as far north of Perth as I do that no one has
ever heard of it.

I'm nineteen years old, and I've been working as a sales rep
for a photocopier business since I left school. I got the job in
December, and my mum was over the moon about it. She said
it was a good, steady job, and the way she said it made me feel
like it was the kind of job I'd still be at in my forties when I'd be
elevated to the lofty heights of middle management. They gave
me a shitty Nissan diesel station wagon, which I thrashed up and
down the coast to Perth, visiting every business and school who
showed the remotest interest in photocopying anything. It always
seemed like some kind of minor miracle when I actually sold one.

At first, I liked having money in my pocket. I didn't realise quite
how shit the wages were, but then I'd never had any money before.
I spent it like water – buying all sorts of crap I didn't need, and
shouting slabs of beer for my mates – but when they buggered off
to university in Perth in February the novelty wore off.

For a while, before each trip down the coast I'd leave the office and go straight home to pick up my surfboard. There were some good spots on the route, and I began to deliberately cancel some appointments to go surfing instead. But three months ago my shithead boss had GPS trackers fitted to all the reps' cars and like an arsehole he'd call if any of us deviated even slightly off course.

A year to the day of getting the job, he called me into his office and showed me a graph on his laptop that demonstrated how badly the sales figures from my area had declined since I'd joined the company. He told me I had an attitude problem and went on and on about how I needed to 'pull my socks up' if I wanted to get anywhere in 'this game'. I couldn't stifle a choking laugh when he said that, and he totally lost it then. He started shouting at me and came around the desk and leaned over me. I guessed it was a technique for asserting dominance that he probably learned about at one of the sales conferences he was always going to. As he yelled, flecks of spit flew out of his mouth and landed on my face and I saw that he knew it had happened and I wiped it away, but he didn't apologise, he just kept spewing his shit.

I looked up into his purple, enraged face and something shifted in me. I stood up and told him to fuck off. He backed away. He couldn't believe it. He gaped like a goldfish, speechless, and before he could figure out what to say to me I turned and walked out of his office. It took me two minutes to get my stuff from my desk and I left. I caught the bus home.

My mum was gutted – she went spare for fifteen minutes solid, and then went straight out and bought the newspaper so I could start looking for another job. But I was suddenly sickened by the idea of staying another day in my shitty town, let alone the rest of my life.

I had just under five grand in my bank account. That night I looked online and found a flight to London with a stopover in Denpasar for sixteen hundred bucks and I booked it without a second thought. I told my mum in the morning and she said nothing. Her mouth went into a hard line, and she stared into her breakfast and then got up and went to work.

She seemed to forgive me a bit over Christmas, but I felt more guilty than ever because it was so miserable – just me and her sitting together eating a rolled turkey roast on our laps and watching telly. I got a friend to drop me to the airport yesterday. I never even called my dad – I hadn't spoken to him in months anyway.

I haven't surfed in three months, and before the bloke at the surf shop talked me into buying the surfboard I was considering not bringing one at all, but now that I'm here, and listening to this lad telling me about his previous trips to G-Land over the years, I feel the return of a familiar buzz.

When I tell him I have a plane ticket to London booked for a week's time and no other plans, his face lights up. He holds up his beer bottle, releases his forefinger from its frosted surface, and points it at me.

"You jammy fucking bastard," he says. "If you're not gone out of here to G-Land by the time I drag my sorry arse out of bed tomorrow morning I'm going to punch you in the face."

He invites me to join him and his mates, but I can see that I'm way too far behind, and I tell him thanks but no. I have a couple more beers on my own at the bar and look up G-Land on my phone. For the rest of the evening, whenever I catch his eye, he grins and points at me, and smacks his fist into his palm.

At 6.30 the next morning I'm at Kuta Reef boarding the G-Land ferry. I'm taking a gamble that they'll have a bed for me, and sure enough when we arrive there's loads of places and I get a plush room at Bobby's Surf Camp. It's pretty flash given we're in the jungle, and it's going to eat through my cash quickly, but as soon as I see the set up out front I don't care. The waves are only two foot, but they're as perfect as I've ever seen. If I can pick the juice out of the coming swell I'll head back to Bali afterwards and save my money by searching out the cheapest place I can find until I leave for London.

Sure enough, the waves turn on the next day. It's not as big as forecast, but it's still a solid six foot, and I'm immediately thankful that it's no bigger. It's just getting light when I walk down to the water's edge. A mauve dawn slowly graduates through burnt orange and nectarine, the waves like gold foil, rippling and furling across the reef. Finally, the sun lifts above the land behind me, and the sea goes teal, and the reef seems to rise, its jewels suddenly studding the sea floor. I walk across the coral and the water is as warm as blood.

There's a wave-hungry crew battling at the top of the point. I watched them all paddle out at first light, and I see them hassling and dropping in on each other, so I leave them to it and sit a hundred metres down the line. It proves a good decision; with all their scrapping they're pushing each other way too deep and every fourth wave claims a scalp and rolls through to me empty, a gorgeous canvas of aquamarine blue. Catching them when they're already in the business of barrelling is tricky, but I'm feeling good – my body is fit and strong from the labouring – and I paddle into them hard, with everything I've got. I realise that I've missed this; the purity of it, the simplicity.

I catch a few mid-size waves, and they're things of absolute beauty; cylindrical, crystalline, sinuous. I simply race them down the line, marvelling at the uniformity of them, the ease.

Then I get brave, and paddle into a wave that's a little bigger, but disfigured by a double-up swell coming at a slightly different angle. It goes funky immediately, and the double-up sucks an alarming amount of water off the reef. I get my arse kicked; I scramble to my feet too early and the bottom drops out of the wave. I drift up into the lip and go over the falls; a zero-gravity, twisting eternity, before I'm slammed down again, sent deep, and my butt hits the reef.

I'm reeling, the wind knocked out of me, and I come up clutching my arse, feeling for damage. Pulling myself onto my board, I strain to look, but it seems I've gotten away with it; there's no bloody smear seeping through my board shorts. I paddle up the point slowly, heading well out into the channel, and then sit for a minute to catch my breath.

Outside, a darkening horizon, shades deeper than I've yet seen, heralds a freak set. I can see the ridges like a distant mountain range. I lie on my board and paddle hard, deeper into the channel; I'm in no mood for another pasting so soon.

The first wave of the set is perhaps a foot bigger, and one of the local Indo rippers manages to get to it, paddling hard, springing to his feet and free-falling down the face. He's like a cat; sure-footed and nimble, unperturbed by the insane drop. He simply knifes up and pulls into a magical-looking cavern. He fizzes by me sporting a toothy grin.

When I crest that wave, I see the next one is of an entirely different species. It has already broken, and the crew at the top of the point are scrambling, caught inside, abandoning their boards and diving for the sea floor.

I race for the channel, shitting myself. The wave is eight-to-ten foot; it's hard to tell. I think I'm in for a savage drubbing, but then the wave seems to pull back, to adhere to the reef a little tighter.

I suddenly realise that I'm in the spot. I'm filled with an impulsive, fatalistic urge that, I have to admit, feels good and frightening at the same time. I've never caught a wave even close to this size. I paddle hard and flat and I'm rising, rising, and the thing is feathering and inside there's a grinding roar as it turns itself inside out. I almost pull back because the kaleidoscopic coral spread across the ocean floor seems to rise, thinning the water at the wave's base.

I can hardly believe that I'm trying to catch this thing, but as I begin to slide all rational thought is rendered irrelevant.

Muscle memory and base instinct take over, and I get in one more good stroke before I spring to my feet.

A freshening offshore lifts spray from the wave face, and for a moment I'm blinded, blinking to clear my vision. The wave rockets me forward with a power I've never felt before and the drop seems endless. My bottom turn is nothing more than a long arc, and then I'm slung along the face at a speed I can scarcely credit. I reset, and trim, and finally get a decent look at it. The wave towers above me, and ahead it lurches out of the ocean as though it might go on forever. I'm too deep, and I think I'm gone, that there's no way I can get myself way along there, out on the face. The great glass slab of its lip blots out the sky, but I manage to pump hard; once, twice, and the board responds beneath me.

I'm low on the face, but the wave throws so hard and square that I don't need to set a highline, and in fact I'd probably lose my edge if I tried. I'm suddenly enclosed in the tube, locked in, a passenger on a rollercoaster. I'm as stiff as a board, in a survival crouch, but there's room enough inside the barrel for my errors.

Then, as I speed through the barrel, something happens. Maybe it's because I realise that there's a chance of an exit, and the possibility sends synaptic signals from my brain to my body; I stand a little taller, reach out with my trailing hand and feel the thrum in my fingers as I touch the face of the wave. A millisecond is all it takes; I'm suddenly connected, filled with knowledge that feels primordial, base. Time seems to slow; this rotating, crystal cylinder seems to stop, to glitch. My body moulds itself to the movement of the tube; my legs and feet act independently, making minute adjustments to the direction, the trim.

Then, like a spell broken, I'm suddenly ejected, skimming across a face that's distorting and warping and about to go dry, and I pull off in a kind of reverie. I don't hoot or say a word; all I can hear is my own breath, coming in short, excited gasps.

Chapter 3

It takes just one week in London to convince me I'd go nuts living here. After Indonesia I can't stand the cold greyness of it, and travelling around on the Tube, descending and then emerging back up from the earth, is wholly unnatural. I'm also freaking because the place is so fucking expensive. I'm down to my last grand, and although I try to mentally add it up, I can't figure how I've managed to spend it all so fast.

I'm staying in a backpackers' in Shepherd's Bush and one night I get on the piss with a Scottish bloke and tell him I'm thinking of going to Edinburgh. He advises me not to bother with Scotland at all, but to get myself immediately to Ireland. He says it's the best craic on the planet, but to be sure to bring an extra liver. It's a measure of my aimlessness that the next day I book a cheap Ryanair flight and the day after that I'm in Ireland. I catch the Aircoach to Dublin Bus Station in the centre of the city and wander out into the streets without any sort of a plan. The city kids snigger at me walking along the streets with my surfboard under my arm.

I get the last spot in a bunk room in a backpackers' hostel, and it's a fun place, with young travellers from all over staying there. I meet a bunch of Italians and Spanish in the kitchen when I'm cooking dinner and afterwards we go out. We wind up at a Temple Bar nightclub, and at the end of the night I have a drunken fumble in the dorm with one of the Italian girls. We're trying to stay quiet, but we get some huffy protests from the others in the room and she slips out back to her own room. I get some dirty looks in the morning and I feel like a fuckwit. I don't see her again.

One of the Spanish lads works at the backpackers', but he's due to leave and he asks the manager if I can have his job. She doesn't seem to care one way or another, so he shows me the ropes the next day. All I have to do is man the front desk. The Spanish fella tells me it's the best way to meet girls, but he's a silver-tongued Lothario. The pay is so bad it's laughable, so I ask the manager to hold onto it for me and pay it at the end of the month so that I'm not tempted to spend it. I buy cans of baked beans for thirty cents and have them for dinner.

I love the Irish immediately – even the little shits who pelt me with stones from behind the wall of the estate near the backpackers'. Usually they're out front, mucking about on the footpath. They're tough-as-nails, street-smart lads who never seem to be at school. One day a German lad comes limping into the backpackers' and tells me that the kids had cut open a soccer ball, filled it with rocks and then asked him to kick it to them. He gets pissy with me for laughing, but I can't help it. One day I go over to them and they don't even pretend that they're going to run away; they just stand and stare at me, their chins defiantly in the air. A lad who can't be more than twelve expertly flicks the butt of his cigarette at my feet.

I don't react. I say gidday and I end up having a good chat with them and then they sell me an eighth of hash for thirty euro. I ask them if they're ripping me off and they fall about laughing.

I've never smoked hash, so I've no idea what to do with it, and the oldest lad, who's about sixteen, shows me how to soften it with a lighter and crumble it over the paper. He takes out his own tobacco and rolls it for me there and then. I leave with a perfectly skinned joint, complete with cardboard filter. Now, each time I pass them, which is a couple of times a day, I stop for a yarn. Sometimes they're cold and angry, others they're funny as fuck.

I get a sense of the divide in the city – the North Dubs versus the rich folks on the other side of the river. The street kids call them D4 heads, and a million other names.

I stay in town for three weeks before I'm over the grimy streets and the incessant rain. Back home, we have awnings over all the city pavements to keep the rain off you, and it strikes me that if any country could do with them it's Ireland. It pisses down all the time and you get drowned the minute you step outside. Yet no one in the city, other than the preppy European backpackers in the hostel, seems to own a raincoat.

Two French boys arrive at the backpackers' carrying surfboards. It's their last day in the country, and that night I get talking to them. They've scored epic waves at a place called Bundoran on the west coast, and in particular at a spot out the front of the town known as the Peak.

I figure if it's going to be wet all the time, then I may as well be at the coast.

I tell the manager I'm quitting and she hands me a little envelope with just over six hundred euro in it and she has me replaced by that evening. The next day I trudge back to the bus station, and board the 11am bus to Bundoran. It takes all day, and it's half five by the time the bus pulls up. There isn't a sinner on the street because it's pissing with rain. It feels like I've arrived in the arsehole of nowhere.

It's too dark to see the sea, but there's a constant onslaught of white noise coming from it. The wind is blowing onshore so hard that the rain tastes of salt.

The bus driver points along the road in the direction of the only backpackers' in town and I battle the wind and rain to get to it. I check in, find my room and dump everything on the floor. I sit on the bed for a while, feeling low and alone.

It's only when I go to the loo that I realise the envelope containing my pay from the backpackers' is no longer in my pocket. I panic and sprint back to my room, and even though I know it isn't there I turn my pack upside down on the bed and wildly rake through my belongings. When reality finally sinks in I sit on the edge of the bed, holding my head in my hands and moaning. I have just over three hundred euro in my wallet, but that's it. The sum fucking total.

The owners of the backpackers' let me use their phone to call the bus service, but at this time of night the office is closed. I'll have to wait until morning.

There's nothing else for it. I stuff sixty euro in my pocket and leave the backpackers' for the pub.

The wind screams in off the sea, driving the rain squalls so hard before it that they sting my cheeks as I run along the footpath. It takes only thirty seconds to get from the backpackers' to the pub, but I'm drenched by the time I reach it.

When I open the door, there's a blast of warmth which carries the scent of beer, and salt and vinegar crisps, and the welcome sound of conversation. It's like finding all the people who've been sheltering from the apocalypse. The place is fairly busy for a Wednesday night, but when I walk in it's like a scene from a Western: everyone stops talking and looks in my direction. To my left there are three lads of about my age sitting on low stools by the fire, and the one with his back to me is the last to turn around. He's tall and slight, with a wild mop of curly hair, big ears and freckles. He looks a bit like a grown-up version of the kid from the *Mad* comics.

He'd been telling a story, and was mid-sentence when he turned. Now he sort of looks to one side, sensing the pause in the room. Then a sudden smile splits his face as he looks at me. His comic timing is impeccable. He taps his wrist with his finger.

"Where the fuck have you been?" he says loudly.

I'm confused for a second, but his pals are grinning at him, and then at me, and then I realise he's messing.

Water drips from my face. My clothes are wet through. I jerk a thumb in the direction of the sea.

"Swimming," I reply, and they all laugh. I walk past them and take a seat at the bar. The barman is an old boy – he looks about seventy – and he takes one look at me, fetches a bar towel and hands it over.

"I'm always amazed at what a man will go through to get a pint," he says, and winks.

I order a Guinness and he sets it down in front of me on a coaster as though it's a masterpiece, and actually it is. I sit watching it, mesmerised by the caramel cascade down the sides of the glass as it settles.

Behind me, I can hear everything the wild-haired lad is saying. He has no filter, no volume control. He's telling his mates about an old Dublin woman who visits her doctor every day without fail.

"She's mental, totally fucked in the head, right," he says. He leaves the T off the end of the word – *righ*.

"But the doctor's a decent skin, right. He humours her. He goes out to her in the waiting room, day after day, and chats to her for a couple of minutes. He puts his hand on her forehead and pretends to take her temperature, and then tells her she's fine. Off she goes, happy as Larry. Every fucking day, right."

Righ. I say it under my breath, just like him.

"Then, one day, she doesn't turn up. They're not too worried, but the day after that she's a no-show again. They think about sending someone to her home to check on her, but no one ever thought to ask her where she lives. They say they'll give it one more day. Then, the next day, here she is again. She wanders in, same as usual, not a bother in the world, sits down in the waiting room.

When the doctor comes out, he says to her: 'Mary, you had us worried. We haven't seen you for three days. Where have you been?'

"'I couldn't come', she says to him. 'I wasn't well.'"

The three of them roar with laughter, and I can't help it; I laugh too.

I hear the scrape of a stool, and then the lad is suddenly beside me at the bar. He taps on the wood with his glass.

"Three pints, please, Pat," he says, and then he turns to me. His eyes are cerulean, mad-looking.

"Howaya," he says.

"Gidday," I reply.

"Oh Jaysus Christ. Are you an Aussie?" His eyes go wide, his jaw drops. The features of his face seem oversized, elastic; flamboyant.

"Yep."

"What the fuck are you doing here, man? Are you lost? Why would you leave that beautiful country to come to this shithole? You must be fucking freezing."

"A little bit," I admit.

"Fuck," he says. "Here I am, trying to get the hell out of here to someplace like where you come from, and ye lot are coming here – voluntarily. I don't fucking get it."

"I guess the grass is greener," I say.

"Well, you got that right, anyway," he says. "But that's about all we have to offer."

He puts out a hand, palm up. His arm is long, slender. Blue veins lattice a path of white skin between the freckles.

"Name's Anto," he says.

Chapter 4

I lose count at seven pints, or maybe it's eight. Pat the barman has locked the door, because it's after 11.30pm. A bunch of people piled in for a late drink which became two, then three, and the atmosphere has changed, charged with a drunken energy.

Earlier, *Who Wants To Be A Millionaire* was playing on the TV, and Pat and his old mates at the bar were calling out the answers and mocking each other mercilessly whenever they got one wrong. A question about Australia came up, and of course they all looked over at me. I gave silent thanks that I knew the answer, and when the bloke on the telly confirmed it they cheered.

It was when Anto came up to the bar for a second time that he found out I was a surfer, and immediately he insisted that I join them – him and Mikey and Brendan. Anto's from Dublin, but Mikey and Brendan are locals. They ask me question after question, and I tell them about my shitty hometown, and about all the breaks nearby. Anto gets me to draw the coastline on the back of a napkin and tell him everything about every single spot.

Mikey and Brendan are good blokes, funny and decent, but Anto is wild, enigmatic. He listens with wide eyes, as though I'm telling him the best story he's ever heard. Every thought in his mind is telegraphed on his face. His excitement builds like a pressure cooker.

When Anto's satisfied that he's exhausted my knowledge of Western Australian surf breaks, he takes over. He's funny as fuck, delivering long diatribes in the manner of the people he's describing. He's a master of mimicry, a student of human behaviour. He starts to mock my accent, and when I say 'ripper' he immediately absorbs it into his vocabulary, splicing it into his conversation.

I can see that Mikey and Brendan are under his spell, and it's not long before I am too.

Up at the bar, the TV has been switched off and one of Pat's friends begins to sing. Anto immediately stands and joins him in a duet across the room. It's an old Irish rebel song, Mikey tells me, and Anto sings it with heart and fire, beating his chest towards the end. They finish, and someone else begins, and then someone else. Pat the barman sings a song that I know from somewhere, and he's halfway through it before I realise it's a tune my mum sometimes hums to herself. I've never once asked her what it was. It's called 'Peggy Gordon'.

Pat's voice is pure and powerful and I actually get a little choked up, but to be fair I'm well pissed at this point. He brings the house down, which fires up the others in the pub, and a dozen more songs are sung before he closes the bar. It's an amazing night; I've never seen anything like it; back home there's a shitty, aggressive vibe in most pubs.

People start to leave. We make a plan to surf the next day. We're all drunk, and Anto leans into me conspiratorially and speaks in an upper-class toff accent.

"May I make the bold suggestion that you stay in town for a spell," he says. "It is my firm belief that you could be well suited to the conditions." His eyes are rolling in his head.

I'd already been thinking the same thing. Besides, I don't have enough money to go anywhere now.

"I'll have to find a job and somewhere to live," I tell him. "I'm pretty skint."

Pat comes over then and tells us to drink up.

"Pat – just the man!" says Anto. "Would you ever employ an Aussie? I know they're probably a bit shit, but this young man here's looking for work."

Pat shoos us outside. The wind's still howling and the noise from the sea is incredible. But the rain has stopped, and we stumble onto the street. Pat stares at me for a while.

"Come back and see me on Monday night," he says, and closes the pub door.

"Fucking sorted," says Anto.

Chapter 5

"Ah, for fuck's sake," says Pat.

I've just finished telling him that, at the pub where I worked for a month when I was seventeen, when we knew we were going to be busy we'd half-fill pint glasses with Guinness and leave them in the fridge until someone ordered one, and then we'd top it off – just so we didn't have to wait for it to settle.

"You heathens," he concludes, laughing.

"No one ever complained," I tell him. "In Australia everyone knows Guinness tastes like shit."

Pat laughs even more, his great shoulders heaving up and down. "That's priceless," he says.

I've been here for two weeks, but he still says I'm useless at it. He has me pour a pint. I sit it up on the bar, and he eyes it carefully.

"It'll do," he says, and then winks at me. "You'd better see if it tastes any good."

I fill a glass with ice and open a Club Orange for Pat, then come around the other side of the bar and we sit on the barstools.

There isn't a soul in the pub, but Pat keeps it open because there's always a few that come in for a late drink.

Mikey told me that there's a rumour Pat used to be in the IRA. Either that, or he sheltered IRA soldiers when the Brits came looking for them. No one really knows, and everyone's too scared to ask, he said. Mikey was thrilled when I told him I saw Pat turn off the TV when the English rugby team played last week.

I pluck up the courage to ask Pat the favour I've wanted to for days; I need two weeks' wages in advance. I'm totally skint. I'm sleeping on Anto's couch, and I wake every morning with a sore back. I want to get a place of my own, but I can't pay for it – the last of my money ran out a week ago. Anto has been paying for everything. I knew the Irish had a reputation for their hospitality, but Anto takes it to a new level. He gets angry when I try to stop him from spending his money on me.

Pat doesn't hesitate.

"Of course you can," he says. He tells me he'll organise it tomorrow, and that's that. He goes around the bar, pulls a fifty out of the till and hands it to me.

"To tide you over," he says, sitting down again.

I start to gush my thanks, but he holds up his hand.

"Please," he says. "Think nothing of it. You're very welcome."

I sit with the fifty in my hand, silently overwhelmed at his kindness. It reminds me of my mum.

He's curious about Australia, asking the questions I might expect from a child: just how dry is it, actually? How often would you see a kangaroo? Can the spiders really kill you? He listens intently as I tell him the answers. He's without ego; has no interest in being heard or telling his own stories, he just wants to listen. He'll listen for hours, and he's like this with everyone. He's endlessly tolerant. I don't know if it's the result of running a pub, or the reason he can stand it.

It makes me laugh how Pat phrases his questions: now, if I was a young man of about your age in Australia, what would I be doing for fun? He's funny as fuck without meaning to be, and often genuinely mystified when I laugh at him.

"What?" he says. "What's so funny?" But I can't explain it to him in any possible way that he'll see the humour in it, too.

I have to push him to get him talking, to tell me about himself. He believes his life is entirely uninteresting. Pat has two businesses; this and the undertakers – that bizarre coupling of enterprises common across Ireland. Drink and death. Genius, when you think about it; too much of one leads to the other, and a good payout from both.

"Why would you want to know about that?" he says, when I ask him what it's like being an undertaker.

"Are you kidding?" I say. "Why would I not?"

Pat tells me he inherited the pub and the undertakers business from his father, who ran it for fifty years before him. His mother died when he was very young, so then it was just himself and his dad, who was a hopeless alcoholic, meaning most days it was up to him to keep everything going. It sounds desperate and lonely to me, but Pat recounts it without emotion. In all his life he's never touched an alcoholic drink, he tells me, for fear that his father's addiction is hereditary.

Pat tells me the story of the time when his father forgot to put petrol in the hearse, spending the money on drink instead, and how it shuddered to a stop halfway down the main street during the funeral procession of a local councillor. It was the biggest funeral of the year. Three hundred people were tailing the car, walking slowly down the street behind it. They were only a short distance from the cemetery.

Pat, at thirteen years old, was in the passenger seat of the hearse, his father driving. When his father realised what had happened, he froze, paralysed by shame and panic. Pat got out, walked around the car and swung open the back door of the hearse.

Pat laughs as he remembers that his voice cracked and warbled as he spoke to the crowd. He told them that as a man of great importance to the town of Bundoran, it would be only fitting that the councillor make his final journey carried high on the shoulders of the people whom he loved and served so selflessly. The men came forward, nodding in agreement, pulled the coffin from the hearse and the procession continued with Pat at its head. His father, mortified, stayed in the hearse, his head down.

Pat tells me that he embalmed his first body at fifteen, entirely on his own, and was all but running the business by the time he left school. Two years later his father was dead of cirrhosis, and Pat was in charge of everything.

"From that day to this," Pat says to me, tapping the bar, "I've only ever had a week off – four days for my honeymoon, and three when my son was born."

It's the first I've heard of a son, and I ask about him.

He tells me that his son was killed along with his best friend four years ago in a head-on collision just outside of Bundoran. The other driver was in his mid twenties, drunk and high.

Pat tells me his son's name was Seamus. He was good at school. The best hurler in the county for his age. Volunteered at St Vincent De Paul on weekends. He could play the flute and the tin whistle, and sometimes played right here in the pub with a crowd of musicians that gather for a session every Sunday. Tears well in Pat's eyes as he talks, and they fall onto his cheeks but he's not embarrassed by them; he doesn't wipe them away.

Pat tells me that his grief at losing Seamus brought him to the brink of taking his own life and nearly destroyed his marriage. It was like driving through pea-soup fog, he says – oppressive and endless – and without any certainty that it would ever lift.

Chapter 6

Anto and I drive to County Clare in my new car. Anto bought me a fucking car. I was getting settled in to my new house, a tiny little place at the end of lane in town, which I just managed to pay the deposit on with Pat's advance, when Anto knocked on the door. He was jumping up and down like a nutter, and he said I had to go with him immediately. He was basically running, and I followed him down the road to the garage, where Anto stopped and pointed to a battered looking old Fiat Punto and told me it was mine, but only if he could use it too. I was dumbfounded, and I tried to tell him that I couldn't accept it, but he just told me to fuck off. He'd even done the paperwork; the car was in my name. It's a shit heap, but it goes.

Anto's mad keen to surf Aileen's, a big-wave spot at the foot of the Cliffs of Moher, but as soon as we get there we can see that the swell isn't anywhere near as big as was predicted. Anto fumes and rages on the clifftop, spewing abuse at the surf forecasters and the weather gods. I'm relieved as hell; I've never seen a surf spot so intimidating. The swell smashes into the base of the cliffs, launching its pulverised foam skyward. The boom of the impact rolls up the cliff face to us.

Instead, we drive a bit further down the coast to Spanish Point, and it's clean and a solid six foot on the outside reef. As we paddle out I realise how heavy the wave is; it's an A-frame that rears and pitches a thick, meaty lip pretty much square, breaking for no more than sixty metres. The surface gushes with boils everywhere and it's immediately clear to me that the tide is way too low. I say as much to Anto, but he ignores me and paddles straight in deep, right to the top of the peak. I can hear him babbling to himself as he goes. It's only the third surf I've had with him, the others being fun, head-high beachies at Tullan Strand. This is a different Anto entirely, I realise. I play it safe, sitting on the edge of the channel, waiting to see if any of the big sets might swing wide and break in deeper water.

Anto lets the first one go, and I think he's realised that it's a bit hairy; it turns itself inside out in a grotesquely misshapen, stepped shambles of a wave. There's nowhere to go but onto the rocks. But the next wave in the set is a bomb, and Anto races out to meet it.

He takes off late, scrambling to his feet, and makes the drop by the skin of his teeth. Behind him, the cavern of the tube churns like a meat grinder. He fades to get into the barrel, but the angle of the wave is weird, and the tube backs off, eluding him. But it's still a good wave; he's slung out onto the face and the wall grows alongside him, and he looks like he's locked into a highline speed run for the rest of it. Instead, Anto fades again, then leans into a savage bottom turn. The wave rears above him. I see him eye the lip. I have a grandstand view of him when he hits it. It's bonkers; it's not a section that should be hit. But he goes vertically up the face and slashes at it with everything he's got, and the wave launches him like he must have known it would. I could see the look on his face when he made the turn: pure anger.

He's right at the part of the reef where it breaks closest to the rocks, and he's annihilated by the wave exploding on top of it.

He's lost from view in the chaos, and when I see him again he's twenty metres further in, being driven by the furious turbulence up onto the kelp and the rocks. I can do nothing to help. When the next wave hits I see him stand and dive into it, his board tombstoning and smashing against the rocks behind him. One more wave goes by before he gets himself clear and into the safety of the channel, and I paddle over to him. He's treading water, examining the remains of his board. There are huge dings and gouges all over it. There's a tear along the side of his wetsuit, up under his arm. When I get close he holds up his hand to me. His little finger is bent at a strange angle; instead of pointing up, it extends across the face of his palm.

"Do you reckon it might be broken?" he asks. There isn't a hint of regret, of fear. He's grinning like a nutcase.

We get ashore and I help Anto take his wetsuit off. Then I strap his little finger to its neighbour with a shoelace.

"Fucking witch doctor," he says, grimacing with the pain as I ease it into place. Then, we set off for Lahinch to find a doctor.

On the drive, Anto starts to talk about his life in Dublin, before surfing. He calls it Anto 1.0. It sounds like a shit-show; never-ending hard knocks and grinding poverty. He knows his dad to see, but has never once spoken to him in his adult life. Once he saw him pissing in the middle of the street, bombed out of his mind.

Anto's the oldest of three, and his childhood was robbed; he looked after his little brother and sister because his mum worked two jobs as a cleaner and wasn't there in the mornings or evenings. He had to cook and clean for them all since he was ten years old.

He got into more and more trouble at school. Then, on the morning of his sixteenth birthday, he arrived at the school gates but walked right past, never to return. His mum went spare, but he refused to go back and she couldn't do anything about it.

Anto tells me he became depressed, and when his mum found herself a decent full-time job and could look after his brother and sister he left home to live in a squat with a bunch of lads he knew from his estate. They'd all left school too, and were making a living selling drugs and stealing car stereos and whatever else they could get their hands on. They'd have huge piss-ups in the squat, drinking and smoking hash until the sun came up.

A few of them started taking smack, and then more of them, and one day when they were sitting watching TV and drinking cans of Tennents and Anto was feeling shitty he relented and let them stick a needle in his arm. He was flattened for hours, sitting there in front of the telly, not speaking to anyone; marooned in the sticky miasma of a heroin trip. He eventually passed out. Anto tells me that when he awoke, he was on his own, the TV still blaring in front of him. The news came on, and there was a two-second teaser clip of a lad riding a giant wave at Mullaghmore. It was so big, he looked like a flea on a dog. Anto sat through the news, waiting for the sport, and for the story to come on.

When he saw it properly – saw the craggy headland of Mullaghmore, the giant, grey-green mountains of water being ridden by those fearless gladiators – something clicked inside him. Adjusted itself. Realigned his path, fired his imagination. He knew immediately what he was going to do. He could see no obstacles at all; he wasn't discouraged by the fact that he had no money, and no means to achieve any of it. He wasn't afraid. Anto laughs when he tells me that up until that point he'd been swimming only twice in his life, and had never gone in past his waist.

He got up off the couch, packed his stuff and moved back home. He found work in a greasy spoon café and in a pub on the weekends and sold hash and pills, mostly to the lads back in the squat. He saved as much as he could. The little time he had to spare was spent researching the best places to surf. He went into the library for the first time in his life because he found out they had two books on surfing.

He enrolled in a swim class, and learned to do freestyle with posh kids half his age. The swim coach was a poncy fuckwit, but he didn't care. Within six months, Anto had bought a second-hand board and a wetsuit and moved to Bundoran. He had just enough to pay the deposit and advance rent on a flat. It was a freezing, crappy bedsit, but from its front window he could see the ocean. It was all he cared about.

Chapter 7

It's getting dark. I've been out for over four hours now, and my shoulders are spent, leaden. The chill has travelled deep inside my body. My neck aches.

When Bren and I paddled out to the Peak, it was two foot, the faces chopped up to shit by a howling offshore. We were barely able to ride them. Now it's six foot and perfectly glassy. We watched in disbelief as the wind dropped and the waves grew, each set bigger than the last. I've never seen anything like it. It was as though someone was twiddling dials, changing the settings.

Anto and Mikey came out an hour ago, fresh from work, hooting and frothing. Anto has his broken finger heavily strapped and he holds it up to show me.

Bren and I laugh at them scratching for every wave that forms on the reef. Some of the local crew get shitty at Anto, but he only mocks them. There's something about the look in Anto's eye and his North Dublin accent that gives people pause before tangling with him. They start to head in, sated by the abundance, and then suddenly it's just the four of us, trading the final waves of the day.

We split the peak. Bren and Mikey surf the right, with Bren gouging great chunks of water out of the tops while Mikey sinuously snakes along the faces and floats long sections with the finesse of a ballet dancer.

Anto and I catch the longer lefts. There are too many waves for just the two of us, and Anto groans at each one that goes by unridden. He takes off ever deeper, folding his angular body into the tubes and sometimes making it, other times eating shit. He goes over the falls on a couple of bombs that light him up pretty badly, but as usual he shakes it off, paddles out again, and is ready for more.

There's a long lull just as the light goes. The four of us bob around out the back waiting to catch one in, not speaking. Anto's further out than me, and he turns to say something, but instead he looks past me and his mouth drops open and he points up at the sky. To the east, the moon has risen over the town, and it looks like a giant pearl, huge and shimmering.

Anto howls at it like a wolf, and Bren and Mikey join him. They yap and howl and laugh, and I'm infected and start to howl too.

This'll do me, I think to myself.

It's almost midnight by the time we get to the nightclub. Anto's on fire. He raged through the town's pubs, and when he's like this we just follow him to see what's going to happen next. Bren has to work tomorrow, so he peels off outside the club and goes home. The sign outside says there's an ABBA tribute band on, and I think it's going to be shit, but the place is absolutely heaving. Half the people there are dressed like ABBA, and there's an air of joyful madness about the place. Anto disappears immediately and is back with an handful of Es before I even make it to the front of the queue at the bar.

"Down the hatch," he says, and he swallows one before holding another out to me. He's completely oblivious to the people around us in the queue – they might as well not be there.

"Your turn," he says. He grins and presses the pill into my hand.

"Fuck, Anto," I reply, and I shove it into my pocket. "Can we perhaps wait until we find a dark corner?"

I buy Anto and Mikey a beer, but by the time I get back to them only Mikey's waiting for me. He points at the dancefloor, and there's Anto jerking around like a maniac, talking to everyone all at once. I grin at Mikey, and we clink bottles.

I fish out the E from my pocket and snap it in two. I swallow half and offer Mikey the rest, but he shakes his head and says he good. Fuck it, I think, and eat the other half. It's bitter, metallic.

Mikey and I watch the band and they're amazing; they're better at being ABBA than ABBA ever was. They suck people onto the dancefloor, powerless to resist.

"Mikey!"

A pretty blonde girl has emerged from the crowd and throws her arms around Mikey's neck and kisses him on the cheek. She's flushed and fizzing with excitement. She's wearing a sequinned minidress, with white boots that come up to her knees. They're covered in jewels. On her head, she wears a carnival headdress with peacock feathers rising up out of it a metre in the air. Mikey smiles at her.

"The dancing queen," he says. "How's it going?"

"Fucking amazing," she says. "They're so good."

"They are," agrees Mikey. He turns to me. "Sam, this is Sinead, my sister. Sinead, this is Sam. He's from Australia."

Sinead turns to me and takes my hand. Her eyes glitter in the lights. She smiles, and I'm immediately drawn in, spellbound.

"Hello, Sam from Australia," she says.

"I love your costume," I say.

She looks at me, her face suddenly serious.

"What costume?" She grins at me, waiting for an answer. But I take too long and she skips away, heading for the dancefloor. But then she turns and looks back at Mikey and me. She has to shout over the music.

"Are ye coming?"

The E hits me half an hour later, and for about fifteen minutes I'm completely mashed. But it doesn't matter, because we're on the dance floor and I sway about with my eyes closed. The tribute band has finished, and a DJ is playing house music that makes my chest pulse with the speakers. The bass is deep and primal, the treble fragile, crystalline. I'm enveloped by it; when I put my hands out it feels like I'm actually touching the music.

Then the E backs off and settles into a warm buzz, and I'm back in the room and I open my eyes and I see Sinead dancing with her friends, but looking over at me. She smiles. She comes over.

"Hello, you," she says, and I smile back. We dance without speaking, and the music is good; loud and driving and insistent. She's a great dancer, physical and fluent. I tell her she dances like Mikey surfs and immediately feel like an idiot for saying it but she just laughs at me.

Later, when the music stops and the lights come on, we stand by the bar finishing our drinks. The bouncers haven't yet started their sweep, and no one wants to leave. Sinead's friends are lovely; warm and welcoming. They're funny as fuck, and the banter goes back and forth like a tennis match. Anto arrives back from somewhere, high as a kite, and he's immediately in the centre of it.

I'm talking to Mikey and Anto and Sinead when a guy comes up behind her and covers her eyes with his hands. He's tall and muscular. There's a harp tattooed on his forearm.

"Guess who?" he says.

Sinead squeals and turns and wraps him in a hug.

"Oh shit! Hello, stranger," she says. "When did you get back?"

"Two days ago," he replies. "I've been posted back here now. I'm staying – I start on Monday."

"That's great news," she says. "Dublin not your cup of tea, then?"

"The criminals here steal sheep – if you're lucky. They're fucking mental over there. I've decided I like the quiet life."

Sinead introduces me. His name is Finbar, and they were best friends right through high school. Now he's a cop – a Garda. They get to reminiscing about their school days, and I turn to Anto, but he's gone.

Chapter 8

Anto's watching a YouTube video of G-Land on his phone when I come out to him. He's in the Fiat, which he borrowed days ago, and he's tied the surfboards to the roof so loosely that they've slipped backwards under the straps and the nose of the topmost board is almost free.

He sees me and winds down the window.

"Look at this," he says. "This was yesterday. And here we are freezing our bollocks off. Fuck."

It's a drone shot of the mechanical Indonesian left-hander draining down the reef. It's big; Anto is only ever interested in big surf.

"Did you get it like this?" he asks, and I nod in reply.

"Fuck. Next year," he says. "You and me and the lads. A month. No – more – two months."

I nod.

"Just say the word," I reply. "I'd go back there any day."

I tighten the straps. There are no racks; the straps just go over the boards and the roof and then pass back through the car doors. I glance at the sky with suspicion; when it rains the water leaks in where the straps part the rubber seal around the doors, and in minutes a steady stream is dripping onto your lap.

I've had to buy another board; mine was snapped in half three days ago during a chunky session at PMPA – a slabbing left-hander south of Bundoran Bay. I tried to do a repair job on the board Anto half destroyed at Spanish Point, but it was beyond my capability so I had to shell out two hundred for a secondhand board which has seen better days. Anto just went out and bought a brand new one. Not for the first time I wondered where he got his money; he barely did any shifts at the gas station.

Worst of all is that now I'm fucked for money again, and it will be three or four more paydays before I can afford a decent new board.

I haven't seen Anto much. I've been hanging out with Sinead whenever I haven't been working. I've fallen hard; she's mesmerising. But I feel like a cheapskate; she's been paying for everything because I'm so broke.

Anto hassles me for information about G-Land even though I've told him loads of times before. He listens intently and wants to know all the boring details; where you fly in, where to catch the ferry. When I describe the wave, he wants to know more; he wants to hear about the take-off, the sections, the imperfections. He nods constantly as I tell him, his eyes on the road, but he's seeing something else, too; he's visualising it. He's banking it, storing it for later use. Anto's always like this about surfing; he has laser focus. He's like the most diligent, engaged student in a classroom.

We're halfway to Gweedore before Anto's thirst for knowledge is sated, and he goes quiet for a while, thinking it over. We stop at a Spar for a breakfast roll and keep going, travelling through the eerie treeless bogland of the northwest.

Then, as though a switch has been flicked, Anto starts to talk again. We're on the way to a spot near Bloody Foreland, where he knows some farmers who'll let us go over their land to surf a right-hand point. Anto discovered it last year when he spent three days driving every boreen in the area and camping in a pup tent each night. He tells me about the farmers: three brothers who never married and are now well into their seventies. When Anto first knocked on their door they invited him inside for a cup of tea and a chat and he reckons it was like going back in time. They had a huge heap of spuds piled on the floor in the corner of the kitchen and when they opened the fridge to get the milk for the tea the only other things in it were a giant ham and a row of beer bottles. The place was manky with years of dirt and dust and Anto couldn't bring himself to drink the tea because the cup was so insanely filthy. They spoke Irish to each other and even when they spoke English it was with an accent so strong Anto had difficulty understanding them.

Anto tells me that when he left the house, one of the brothers came out with him to show him the farm track leading to the beach. They had a bit of a natter, and the brother told Anto the story of what happened the week before when the oldest of the three, who was a raving alcoholic, went to the pub – the same as he has every night without fail for the last fifty years.

Anto can't stop laughing as he tries to tell me the story. "Wait till you hear this," he says. "This night, says your man, the older brother took himself off to the pub as usual, and he got himself absolutely twisted by closing time. The staff of the pub are well used to him, and they call him the only taxi in the area. Now this taxi is driven by another old lad, who's been driving this brother home for twenty years himself. When the taxi arrives, the bar staff help the brother into it and then go back inside to clean up the place and have a pint themselves. Then, when they're finished, they lock up the pub and leave but when they get outside they see the taxi is still in the carpark with the engine running. What the fuck, they think, and they go to investigate."

Anto can barely tell the story at this point; tears are streaming down his face. I'm laughing too, thoroughly infected by him.

"Ah, jaysus christ," says Anto. "Oh fuck. This country is the best. So they go out to the car and open the door and your man is sound asleep on the cabbie's shoulder, snoring like a pig."

"What the hell?" I say, confused, and Anto cracks up again.

"Yeah. That's what they said," he replies. "So they try to talk to the cabbie, but he doesn't reply, and then they go around to his side and open the driver's door and out he slumps. He's dead!"

Anto has to slow the car because he's laughing so hard; he swerves and wobbles across the road. "He's had a fucking heart attack! Oh fuck, oh jaysus," he says and the story is funny but Anto telling it is even funnier and I'm caught up and before long my chest is hurting and we actually do pull over.

When we get to the farm, Anto runs inside but he's out again in a jiffy – the old boys aren't there. He says they won't mind, so we go past the house and a stone-walled shed filled with dilapidated farm equipment that looks as though it hasn't been used in years. I open the gate and Anto guns the Fiat to get through a mud patch. It fishtails and slithers but he makes it and I leap in again and from there it's a five-minute white-knuckle ride to the beach. Anto sends the car into enormous puddles without slowing, and some of them are so deep we make a bow wave and Anto has to put on the wipers.

"Fuck yeah," he bellows, and the engine screams as we go up the last rise before the beach and finally come to a stop at the end of the boreen. We get out and Anto runs up a little hill to get a view of the beach. I follow him.

The wind is strong and offshore and I can see straightaway that there's no shortage of swell, but for a moment I think we've blown it; a big, scrappy closeout rumbles through the centre of the beach, shapeless. But then a set rears on the horizon and we watch as it forms off the headland at the north end. The wind is from the northeast, and the tops of the swells are studded by whitecaps. But by the time the first wave reaches the lee of the headland, the chop has gone, and it transforms into a smooth-backed monster. As if by magic, like some giant rope is drawing it upwards, the wave rises at the end closest to the headland, rearranging itself into an A-framed tepee. We watch, enthralled and speechless, as it folds over, the left pulverising itself on the rocks of the headland, the right forming a barrel so square I'm instantly thrilled and terrified at the same time. It's eight-to-ten foot. It throws and throws, cranking down the line in a continuous, violent detonation of whitewater. I can see jets of water spurting through the back and into the air, forced like malfunctioning pistons through the wave by the pressure created inside the collapsing barrel. There's a rushing, voluminous spit, which blows out of the barrel and twists up, whipped away by the wind. But the wave continues and, incredibly, does it again.

"Oh yes! Oh fuck yes!" shouts Anto, and he throws an arm around me and jostles me about. "What did I tell you, you little fucking beauty?"

We're into our wetsuits and in his hurry Anto leaves his clothes scattered on the grass around the car. We run over a ridge of loose stone on our way to the beach, and it's only when I come down the other side that I realise the ferocity of the shorebreak; it's a steep beach, and there's a mutant, stepping closeout breaking right onto the pulverised shingle, which hisses and roars as it's dragged up and down the beach.

"It's not hard getting out," says Anto cheerfully. "But just wait until you try to get back in."

He sprints down the sand and throws himself belly first onto his board and skims out across the water. I think he's made a horrible mistake because there's a solid wave approaching. It sucks back off the beach so hard it stands the wave up vertically, and for a moment it's a double overhead grey-green wall. Somehow Anto manages to squeak through it. I half expect to see him sprawling on the sand, sucked back with it, but when the curtain of spray recedes I see him out past the danger zone, looking back at me, grinning as he theatrically mimes wiping the sweat from his brow.

I take a more cautious approach and wait for a lull, but it's still a frightening experience and my breath is coming in short, sucking gasps by the time I realise I'm safely beyond the shorebreak.

Anto's well ahead of me now, but I can still hear him hooting and screaming at every single wave that reels down the point towards us. They're freight trains, breaking along the submarine ledge so fast I'm not sure if they're even makeable.

Of course, Anto's the first to find out. As soon as he reaches the take-off point, a huge set looms, and without hesitation he swings and goes on the first one. It rears and pitches so quickly that he's pulled up the face, right to the top, and the drop is the most critical thing I've ever witnessed. He falls out of the sky, and the wave is perhaps two and half times overhead when he finally makes it to the bottom. He screams out onto the flat, his board chattering under his feet, and I can see that he's struggling to hold on. When finally he gets it together enough to make a bottom turn I think that it's too late; that he's going to wear the lip on the head. Instead, incredibly, he sneaks beneath the falling curtain and is suddenly cocooned. It looks like a giant slab of jade – milky green and streaked with marbled spume.

Somehow, Anto's botched bottom turn has set him up perfectly for the yawning chasm of the barrel, and I see him drift up high on the face and then he's flat to the boards, a bullet in a gun barrel. He's ridiculously deep, and I lose sight of him as I pass over the wave. I turn and watch, and I keep on expecting him to pop up in the boiling foam. The wave runs and runs, and way down the line Anto suddenly appears again, planing over the back of it. He stays standing as his board loses speed and he begins to sink – he's charged, triumphant. I hear his guttural howl over the roar of the surf.

Anto's always telling me he wishes he started surfing as a kid, like I did. He says he wishes he could surf like me. But today he out-surfs me in every way. He takes off deeper, makes barrels that defy belief. He catches three times as many waves as me, and takes a mad amount of beatings, some so brutal that I worry he won't come up. Twice he gets pinned to the rock underwater, and held there for an uncomfortably long time by the downward force of the lip. Each time he paddles straight back out, hungry for more.

I'm cautious throughout; I don't blow a single take-off, but I don't get barrelled either. I wish like hell I had my own board. Every wave is a mad rush; an adrenaline-filled speed run, but I know I haven't made the best of it. I know I'll lie awake tonight thinking of it.

Then, just as Anto and I nod to each other and say 'one more', I catch and ride the best wave of my life. The waves have begun to back off as the tide comes in; they're starting to mush a little bit. Only the monsters are still tubing, and I don't want much to do with them.

But I crest a wave and see that the next one is an absolute bomb; ten foot and flawless. Anto's paddling back out, almost at the take-off zone, and he bellows at me, calling me into it.

I'm sitting right in the spot. I couldn't be better positioned. I know he'll be disgusted if I let it pass. The thought of disappointing him wrestles with my fear, then overcomes it.

With my heart in my mouth I put my head down and go. I paddle early and hard, but even so I'm near the top when I get to my feet. The drop is appalling, endless, breathtakingly fast. I'm as tense as fuck – rigid and standing bolt upright, knees locked – but I'm blessed by an unfathomable kindness: the wave face is unblemished glass. There are no ribs, no chop. The wind has completely died away.

I lean into a drawn-out, arcing bottom turn; my instinct for self-preservation forces me to retain all the speed I possibly can. I'm flying now, and with the drop behind me I'm suddenly filled with confidence, with bravado. The hard part is over.

I hear Anto shout at me as he passes over the wave, and the thought actually goes through my head that with this one wave – this one bomb – I've gained his approval. Whatever happens, he saw me stroke into it, and that's enough.

But he's yelling because he knows what's coming. He's had half a dozen of these.

I'm in control. My board is singing beneath me. I can feel through my whole body the immense, boundless power of the wave.

But milliseconds too late I realise that the face is changing, warping, beginning to rear alarmingly far down the line. The wall suddenly grows and stretches away from me. I pump desperately, but I only get a couple in before I know I'm lost. I'm way too deep. If I'd stayed focused, I'd have seen it coming, pumped earlier, set a highline for speed, and maybe I might have made it. But now I can only watch helplessly as I'm overtaken by the rotating maelstrom of the barrel. I think about stepping off straight away – to attempt a pin drop through the face – but it's too late for that, too, and the truth is I'm too afraid. I'm paralysed by indecision. There's no doggy door, and no way I'll make it out. I'm travelling at warp speed, and I wait for the impact, for the tube to constrict, or the foam ball to mow me down. The opening recedes and recedes, impossibly far ahead, like a portal to another world. Yet, somehow, my headlong rush through the tunnel continues, a second turning into two, into three, four.

I feel the spit before I see it; a blast of wind and spray that blows my hair over my face, swings my arms forward. The power of it is incredible, and suddenly I can't see a thing for the spray. I'm on the very edge of control, my heels hard on the rail, fighting for purchase in the face. But my sudden loss of vision forces a kind of resignation in my body. I give in, expecting to be skittled, and I know that I'll need to stay calm to hold my breath for the inevitable wipeout. Yet it doesn't come. Somehow I travel through the barrel still, and when the spray clears I see that I'm metres closer to the opening than I was. The wave seems to breathe, to pause, and the effect is to change the shape of the tube – an oval, then an almond. It's clamping, pinching, and I rise on the face, and compress, my body now making decisions of its own accord. The exit is suddenly tiny, but I fly out of it like a cannonball, busting through the chandeliers dropping from the ceiling.

I can't believe it; I'm back out on the face, and the wave is broadening. A carpet of foam settles over its back like sheep's wool thrown by a rousey. It foams and spritzes, then dissipates into nothing more than spume-streaked ocean. I'm dumbfounded, and I sit down on my board and let it sink in.

I turn and look back to the top of the line-up in time to see Anto catch the last wave in the set. He's dialled in; has the wave sussed. He doesn't crouch for his bottom turn, but stands tall, then arches his back. He snaps hard under the lip and sets up for the barrel like he's been doing it all his life. It isn't the monster mine was, but he gets well and truly shacked for a few seconds and emerges from the barrel like a gorilla, his shoulders hunched, his arms hanging loose by his sides. He looks back at the tube, watches its eye close. He pumps along the fattening wall right through and pulls off beside me. His face is aglow. He grins madly.

"Some fucking buzz, man," he says, and we high-five like little kids.

On the way home, we've only gone as far as Bunbeg when Anto says he has to make a stop but he won't tell me any more than that; he just taps the side of his nose and grins. He says he has an hour to kill and we're ravenous, so we stop at the pub and get steak and chips and a pint each. When we come out, it's dark and the wind has turned to the north and it's freezing cold. Flecks of flying sleet can be seen in the streetlight.

We get back in the car, but instead of turning onto the main road, Anto heads towards Bunbeg Wharf.

I ask him again where we're going, but he doesn't answer. He's quiet, staring straight ahead. There's a car parked up at the entrance to the pier, and as we pass I can see four teenagers inside. A puff of smoke billows out of their half-open window. A fisherman is tidying up his nets at this end of the wharf, and down at the other I can just make out a couple walking their dog.

"Fuck," says Anto under his breath. "Grand Central Station."

Anto spins the car around in a U-turn and drives a hundred metres away from the pier. He parks in the shadow of the buildings and winds down the window. I think he's looking out across the black water to the cliffs on the other side, then realise that he's actually staring into his wing mirror, looking back down the pier. He's jumpy, anxious. He mumbles something I don't hear. He keeps checking the time on his phone.

"Anto, what the fuck are we doing here?" I ask him. I leave him in no doubt that I want an answer this time.

"I'm picking something up," he replies. "A package."

He stops, and I sit, staring at him, waiting silently for him to continue.

"It's a fucking package," he repeats. "I receive it, bring it to Dublin, get paid. That's it. It's a courier service."

I nod slowly.

"And what's in it, Anto?" I say. My chest feels tight.

But he's watching the couple with the dog ambling slowly back up the pier.

"Come on, you fuckers," he says quietly.

"Anto?"

He suddenly turns on me.

"What do you think, Sam? Don't be a fucking baby," he says.

Anto gets out of the car and slams the door. He walks back down towards the pier. I turn and watch him. He passes the couple with the dog, nodding politely at them. Then he walks up to the car with the teenagers in it, and I see him bend down to talk to them through the window. He's talking and gesturing in the direction of the wharf, and then he points back towards me. I see them all turn around to look. Then Anto straightens up and walks away. I can't imagine what he said to them, but immediately I see the brake lights of the car come on and then they're moving; U-turning and coming back past me. They glance at me as they drive past.

I'm stunned, aghast at Anto's recklessness. Things suddenly make sense; his mystery disappearances, why he's been flush with cash, buying boards and shouting rounds of tequilas at the nightclub. He's been working less and less at his job at the service station. Two weeks ago he gave me a hundred euro and told me to fuck off when I said I'd pay him back.

But I'm furious that he's involved me. I should slide over to the driver's seat and start the car and drive home; just leave him here. But I'm rendered useless by fear and indecision. I simply sit here, swivelled awkwardly in my seat, watching Anto walk down the pier. He's halfway along it when I see the moving lights of a fishing boat out in the harbour. It's travelling quickly, and I see Anto begin to jog in order to meet it at the end of the pier.

I lose him in the gloom and distance, but it's only minutes before the lights of the boat appear alongside the wharf and soon after that I see Anto coming back. His hands are shoved into the pockets of his jacket in an attempt to hide the bulge underneath. He's walking, but I see him break into a jog again when he gets off the pier and a stab of fear shoots up my spine. When he's fifty metres away I finally decide to slide over and start the engine. I don't turn on the headlights. Anto makes for the driver's side, but when he hears the engine he comes instead to the passenger side and jumps in. I drop the clutch and we're away before he's even closed his door. I only turn on the headlights when we get up the road a bit.

"Getaway driver, huh?" says Anto, and he grins but I don't look at him. I keep my eyes on the road.

Anto keeps swivelling to look out the back window of the car, but when we get back onto the main road I see him visibly relax. He bangs the roof of the car with his hand.

"Done deal," he says.

"Fuck you, Anto," I reply.

He tries to apologise. I don't even answer him. He's silent for ten minutes, but then he starts babbling, telling me how much he makes for doing a pickup, and how fucking easy it is. He says that he'll cut me in if I help him – drive, or keep a lookout. We'll be in G-Land in no time, he says. There's another pickup ten days from now at Teelin Wharf.

The whole time I don't say a word.

But then I start to think about that new board, about the fee for a visa extension that the Irish immigration department emailed me about last week, how I can't ask Pat for another advance on my pay.

When he drops me home I open the boot to pull out my wetsuit. He swivels in his seat.

"Oi," he says. "Not a word to anyone, right?"

Chapter 9

The end of Teelin Pier ghosts in and out of the fog, as though it has become detached from the land. The water swells around it, its surface like black glass. A single streetlamp halfway down the pier is all the illumination available. It feels like the end of the earth.

But Anto points and I squint and then I can see it; the red port light of the fishing boat glimmering in the inky blackness of the open sea. It's already rounded the headland and soon I can hear the noise from its engines throbbing across the water.

Anto and I are tucked into a space among the rocks, and we keep standing up and looking around, like meerkats emerging from a hole. We've parked the car up the road. We haven't seen a soul since we arrived half an hour ago, but my nerves are still on edge.

The fishing boat chugs into the harbour at full power, and its crew doesn't turn on its floodlights. Within minutes it's rounded the end of the pier and then Anto and I come out of our hiding place and jog down the road and onto the pier to meet it.

It's all over in a few minutes. The captain of the boat brings it alongside, fast, then throws it into reverse and the air vibrates with sound and the backthrust turns the sea to foam. There's a man dressed entirely in black standing outside the wheelhouse, and he bends down as they come alongside. I think he's reaching for a rope for the dock pilings, but instead he picks up a gear bag at his feet.

"Jack Sparrow," he says to Anto.

"Captain Haddock," replies Anto, and the man nods and tosses the bag to him.

Immediately, the boat swings away from the wharf, and circles tightly around in the harbour. The captain opens the throttle, the boat gathers speed, and within thirty seconds it's gone, steaming past the end of the pier.

"Easy fucking peasy," says Anto as we walk back to the car, but I'm hyperventilating.

On the trip back to Bundoran, I realise there's a tremor in my hands. It takes a long time for them to still as the adrenaline slowly leaves my body. Anto doesn't notice. He's on a high; charged with the thrill.

"It's payday tomorrow, my friend," he says, and he stops and rolls a spliff to celebrate. We get out and smoke it by the side of a lonely road. It's pitch black, and not a car comes past us the whole time.

When we get back on the road, despite my protests Anto opens the bag and pulls out five packages. He lays them across his lap and then whistles as he weighs them in his hands.

"So fucking much," he says.

Finally he zips them back into the bag and starts to talk. He's going on about what he's going to do with the money; he talks about G-Land again. He tells me he's saving up, but he's probably talking bollocks. He's been spending money like it's water.

I'm quiet, stoned, a bit haunted by what we've done. The spliff was definitely a bad idea – my paranoia is peaking. It seems to imbue the package in the boot with a palpable weight; it sucks the energy from the car. For the first time I start to think about the people who will end up hoovering the coke up their noses. I try to think, instead, about what I'll do with the money but the guilt crashes in on me.

It's almost 10pm by the time Anto drops me home. He tells me that he'll pick me up at 2pm tomorrow for the drive to Dublin. I walk down the lane, and get a fright when I see that my lights are on, but it's just Sinead, sitting in my lounge with a cup of tea, watching TV and waiting for me. There's a chocolate wrapper on the table. She's wearing slippers and my jumper, and she looks so cute that I lie down on the couch and put my head in her lap. She kisses me and strokes my hair and asks me where I've been. I say with Anto, surfing, mucking about.

We lie like that until the credits roll on the movie.

I'm still a bit stoned, and stressed, and for some reason I end up telling her where I've been, what I've been doing.

She sits quietly and listens. She stops running her fingers through my hair. But I keep talking, telling her everything – that Anto's done it a few times; that it's safe, it couldn't be easier. I tell her I'll take her on holiday with the money. I don't look at her, but away to the far corner of the lounge. It makes it easier to say. It actually feels good to get it off my chest. Finally, I stop talking, and I look at her, trying to gauge her thoughts. After a moment, she lifts my head and eases out from under me and stands up. She takes her teacup to the kitchen and when she returns she stops in the middle of the lounge. The silence fills the space like an expanding balloon in a confined space, crushing everything around it. I sit up.

"You arsehole," she says simply.

"Sinead…" I begin, but there's nothing else to say. Telling her seems to have laid it out bare, enlarged it, so it can be seen for what it is. I suddenly realise how fucking stupid I've been.

Sinead presses her hands to her face, hard. She makes a sound; a strangled sort of cry. I get up and try to put my arms around her but she pushes me away and yells into my face.

"Don't touch me, you fuck!" she screams, and I reel backwards as though I've been hit. "I can't believe you'd fucking do this, that you'd risk everything – what's the matter with you?"

I can't speak, can't find anything to say. Sinead paces around the lounge a bit, and then she rips off my jumper and throws it on the floor and she finds her shoes and coat and puts them on. I see a tear fall from her cheek when she bends over and it's like I've been punched in the stomach. I say I'm sorry, but she ignores me. She walks to the door, flings it open and is gone.

Chapter 10

When they smash in my front door the noise makes me jerk so violently that I almost fall out of bed. I get up quickly, disoriented and confused. A black fuzz clouds my vision and I stumble and have to steady myself against the wall. Then my bedroom door bursts open and a powerful torch light shines into my face. Involuntarily I crab madly backwards away from it. But I'm not quick enough, and I'm collected in a rugby tackle. The full weight of the man drives me into the floor and there's a sudden, searing pain across the ribs on my right side. Then I'm turned over and pinned down, my face ground into the carpet by a powerful hand.

"Clear," says the man on top of me, and I'm lifted up off the floor and thrown back onto my bed. I curl into the foetal position and brace for an impact; an iron bar, or a bullet, but nothing comes.

The torch is beamed into my face, so I can see little apart from the two figures now standing silently in my room. My breathing is ragged and rapid, quickened by adrenaline.

There are footsteps in the hallway.

"In here, sir," says one of the men, and it's when the beam swings away to the floor I see in the reflected light that they're wearing the uniform of the Gardai – the cops – and I know I'm fucked.

A third man is framed in the doorway, and the officer at the back stands to one side to let him by, then leaves, returning to the lounge.

"Here he is – El Chapo," says the newcomer. He has a North Dublin accent; same as Anto's. He isn't wearing a uniform – just jeans and a jacket and a baseball cap. "So you're the man keeping me from my missus tonight, are you?"

I say nothing, but sit up and lean against the headboard, drawing the covers over me like a shield. My ribs hurt like fuck; every time I inhale pain rips across my torso. My bedside clock glows 4am.

He takes the torch from the officer and keeps it trained on me. He's observing. Calculating.

"I take it you know why we're here," he says.

I shake my head.

"No idea," I say.

He smiles.

"God loves a trier, I suppose," he replies. "My name is Detective Sean Riley from the National Drugs and Organised Crime Bureau. Heard of us?"

I shake my head again, and this time he laughs out loud. He speaks to the uniform.

"Jaysus. I work my arse off, and this is the recognition I get?" he says.

The detective sits down on the edge of my bed. He turns the torch away, placing it down on the blankets, pointing at the wall. Now I can see his face; he's balding, gaunt, his hollowed-out cheeks giving him the appearance of a skull in the torchlight.

"Tell me about yourself, Sam," he says. "Pretend we're on a date."

My scalp prickles. I find my voice.

"Why?" I say.

The detective smiles.

"That's not very forthcoming," he replies. "Especially now that you and I are officially in a relationship."

The officer behind him grunts with amusement.

"I'm hoping it's beginning to dawn on you just how much shit you're currently in," he continues. "And that's only with us. I'd hate for the crowd you're dealing with to find out you've been spending the night with me."

I say nothing in reply, but his words travel through me like poison, chilling my blood.

"We're going to make a deal, you and I," he says. "Essentially, I tell you what to do, and you do it. It's a bit like a marriage."

The officer chuckles again.

"Ugly fucking wife," he says.

"Oh – I'm ugly, all right," says Detective Riley. "And demanding. Nag, nag, nag. I never let up. I'm on you day and fucking night. Where you've been, who you're with… You'll have to tell me everything before I'll leave you alone." The detective cocks his head and looks at me thoughtfully.

"Here's a question: how, in the name of jaysus, did you get yourself into this? You're a foreigner. You should be drinking pints and shagging our birds and writing postcards home to your mammy about the wonderful cultural experiences you're having. Instead, you spend last night at Teelin Wharf, waiting for a shipment of drugs."

My hair stands on end. I can't think; a buzz, a static, fills my head.

"Fuck, man, I'll hand it to you – you've got balls," continues Riley.

"Or he's just fucking stupid," suggests the officer.

The detective nods slowly.

"Or he's just fucking stupid," he echoes.

He stands up.

"The delivery is tomorrow?" He glances at his watch. "Well, later today?"

I nod.

He smiles.

"Now you're getting the hang of it. You're to tell Officer Mahoney here everything you know. I, meanwhile, am going back to bed."

Detective Riley blows me a kiss.

"Night, night, sweetheart."

He turns and walks out of my bedroom.

Two hours later the uniformed officers get up from the kitchen table to leave. Mahoney's as grumpy as fuck because I haven't been able to tell him anything new. Somehow they already know about Anto, but they won't tell me how they found out. I have to assume the only reason they haven't tried to recruit him as their undercover snitch too is because they figure he's likely to tell them to go fuck themselves and do the time in prison. When I asked how they found out about me, Mahoney just smiled and told me I didn't choose my associates very wisely.

They wanted to know the name of the drug dealer that Anto and I are delivering the gear to, and I have no idea so they showed me a bunch of pictures of Dublin gangsters. They all have nicknames: Peter Rabbit, Paddy Knuckles, the Merchant. None of them mean anything to me; Anto hasn't told me shit. The cops have been watching them for a long time, but they're really after the players who supply them – a UK-based gang who send the drugs to Ireland on planes, ferries and fishing trawlers.

My instructions are to observe everything I can tomorrow. I told them I probably won't be making the drop, that I won't even get past the front door, but Mahoney ignored me. He told me to insist that I go inside with Anto. I'm to take note of security measures and methods of communication, make a mental map of the property. When Mahoney said that I should try to take a photo or get a video of the place on my phone, I laughed out loud, which pissed him right off. I'm to listen for information regarding future shipments. Then, I'm to call Detective Riley as soon as I can afterwards. He put the number in my phone under 'Sean'.

The two of them fold up their notepads and Mahoney shoves his laptop into his bag and yawns. He looks at me for a while, then leans down and places his palms on the table.

"If you're not in touch with Detective Riley by the end of play tomorrow you'll find yourself in Portlaoise Prison faster than you can believe," he says. "They fucking love foreigners in there."

I don't reply, and I don't get up from the table. They leave the front door wide open, and through it I can see the grey hue of dawn, feel the cold rushing in. I sit and let it wash over me until I start to shiver. I close and lock the door, then crawl back into bed. My head should be racing, but I feel only a numbness. In a supreme act of cognitive dissonance, I fall asleep.

Chapter 11

"'This car has gone to the dogs.'"

Anto pulls off some of the peeling trim from the dashboard and flicks it at me.

"Look at it, Sam," he says. "It's a fucking disgrace. As its owner, you should be ashamed of yourself. You've let us all down. I'm fucking morto having to travel in it. Talk about Shitty Shitty Bang Bang."

I've barely spoken a word for most of the trip so far, turning everything over and over in my head. I can't look at him, afraid that the look on my face will give it all away. I'd gone to bed determined to tell Anto the next day that I'd finished, that I won't be going to Dublin with him, that I won't be doing any more pickups. I'd lain there, planning what I was going to say to Sinead. I was going to beg for her forgiveness. Instead, I'm fucked; a fly in a trap.

I'm beyond exhausted. My ribs hurt, and a sharp dart of pain goes through me whenever I take a deep breath. I try to hide it from Anto. His banter is a welcome distraction.

"You want to walk, smartarse?" I say.

"It would be faster," he replies. "I'll bet you a hundred euro you can't get this heap up to one fifty."

I floor it. Anto screams and beats the roof. He winds down the window and slaps the side of the Fiat like it's the rump of a horse and lurches about in his seat as I try to hit his target; the engine whines in protest as the needle creeps up painfully slowly; one thirty, one forty, one forty-five. I let out a roar when it finally reaches 150km/h and Anto kills himself laughing as we slow again.

"Zero to a hundred in forty-five seconds, what?" He says. "What a fucking performance machine."

"Who's a good girl," I say, patting the top of the steering wheel like it's a dog.

But it's an act. I fall silent, and the weight of worry crashes down again.

Shitty Shitty Bang Bang makes it to Dublin in under three hours and Anto directs me through the narrow streets on the north side of the city centre. I ask him where we're going and when he tells me that we're meeting someone known as 'the Merchant' I freak, laughing nervously, involuntarily, trying to hide my recognition.

"I know," says Anto, oblivious. "What a wanker. It gets worse. He used to call himself 'the Merchant of Menace' but he must have realised it made him sound even more like a douchebag so now he's just the Merchant. His real name is Darren. Darren! Fucking eejit."

Anto falls quiet. He doesn't crack any more jokes. It's grimy and grey and freezing outside and the light leaches from the sky in the west. We park outside a kebab shop and the guy inside looks up from his phone and stares at us for a long time.

Anto reaches over into the back seat and grabs the gear bag.

"Wait for me," he says.

"No way," I reply. "I'm coming. Safety in numbers."

He looks at me.

"Might be best if you don't…" he says, but I cut him off.

"Forget it," I say. "I'll sit here like a fucking muppet, will I? Have myself a kebab? Either I'm in or I'm out, Anto."

Anto puts up his hands. He looks at me keenly, his eyes narrow, questioning.

"OK," he says. "Keep your hair on. Let's go."

Before I can say anything else, he gets out and slams the door behind him.

I watch him cross the road, shouldering the pack as he goes. I swear under my breath, get out of the car and lock it. There's an icy wind blowing around the streets but I'm suddenly hot, and I pull at my collar which feels like it's choking me. I jog to catch up with Anto and he says nothing, but smiles grimly at me.

We go left and then right and then down behind a row of shops in a service alley, where we stop outside a stone wall with a glittering forest of glass shards cemented along its top. There's a tangle of barbed wire over a steel door and Anto bangs on it and stands back so he's in view of a security camera on a pole behind the wall. We wait for more than a minute before we hear footsteps behind the wall and the metallic shriek of the bolt being drawn back. The door swings open and a tall, skinny lad of about our age steps out. He clocks Anto and gives me the once over before scanning the alley.

"Look what the cat dragged in," he says, and he sounds just like Anto.

"Howaya, Johnny," says Anto, and we step inside. Johnny bolts the door behind us and grins.

"You still riding them waves, Anto? Prefer birds, meself," he says.

"Do you, now?" says Anto in mock disbelief. "Since when?"

Johnny laughs, but there's a hollow ring to it, and still looking at Anto, he asks: "Who's your friend?"

"Sam, Johnny. Johnny, Sam," Anto responds. He doesn't look at me either, but keeps his eyes on Johnny.

"He'll have to stay outside," says Johnny.

"No, he won't," says Anto simply.

Johnny glares at Anto for a while, waiting for him to make his argument, but Anto says nothing. Johnny pats us both down, and then tells us to wait. He goes up the three stairs to the entrance and knocks, and after a moment the door swings open. I can't see who's inside, but Johnny says something to someone and then the door closes and we wait in silence until it opens again. It seems I've been granted access.

The hallway we enter is sparse and brightly lit and there's another security camera at the far end, above another steel door. There's a large man standing in front of it, and the sight of him sends a ripple of panic through me. He's wearing a black leather jacket which he can't zip right to the top because his neck is so huge; wider even than his bull-like, bald, scarred head. His hands are enormous and covered in blotchy blue tattoos. I fight to stay calm, to breathe evenly. He watches us impassively as we walk down the hallway, and doesn't say a word. When we reach him, he turns and knocks on the door and it swings open and we go by him, but his gaze is firmly on me as I pass. He follows us inside and closes the door and stands in front of it, his feet apart, one hand crossed over the other, like a bouncer outside a nightclub.

It's hard to see much inside after the dazzling light of the hallway, but as my eyes adjust I make out what looks like the living room of a student flat. A haze of smoke fills the air. It's humid and smells of fried food and sweat.

There are couches around the walls, a stained carpet, and a broken lamp lying on its side. Two huge black speakers sit on either side of the TV, which is on, but the sound is muted. There's a low coffee table covered in ashtrays and strands of tobacco, bits of cling film and Rizlas, and in the centre there's a large bong with water the colour of long-brewed tea in the bottom of it. Beside it are a spoon and a length of rubber tubing.

An emaciated lad who looks like he could be a cancer patient is laid out on one of the couches, and as he turns to look at us I see that his pupils are tiny pinpricks lost in the expanse of his irises. His arm trails off the couch and as I follow the line of it I spot the needle on the filthy carpet.

Another guy is on his knees in front of the coffee table, and swipes his arm across it, brushing the detritus to the ground.

Sitting back on one of the couches is a third man. He's older – maybe forty. He's wearing a white old-man's singlet, and his arms are muscular and wiry and black with tattoos which disappear under the singlet and re-emerge on his neck. He clasps his hands before him, fingers together, like the evil boss in a spoof spy movie. He doesn't lift his head until the man has cleared the table and taken away the bong. When he looks up I see that his eyes, too, are pinheads, but there's a cold clarity to them. I twig that he must be the Merchant.

"This is irregular, Anto," he says, but he looks directly at me as he speaks. I try to hold his gaze, but my scalp is prickling with fear, and I feel weak. I look at the ground.

"If it wasn't for him we'd all be empty fucking handed right now, Darren," replies Anto. "He saved the day."

"What the fuck are you on about?" says Darren.

"The cops turned up, didn't they?" says Anto angrily.

Anto's lie feels like a hand reaching into my chest and gripping my heart. My breath catches in my throat and my tongue suddenly feels as though it's filling my mouth.

Irritation flashes across Darren's face.

"You still got the gear?" he asks. He taps the table in front of him.

Anto looks grim as he unzips the gear bag and begins pulling out the parcels. He puts them on the table with a slowness that's almost comical. At first I'm confused, but when I glance back and see that the man in the leather jacket is holding a gun I realise that Anto is deliberately moving slowly.

The parcels go on the table – one, two, three, four – and I wait to see Anto's hand reach into the bag again but instead he holds his palm up to Darren.

"That's it," he says to Darren. "We lost one."

I can't help myself; I look at Anto. The shock must be written all over my face. But Anto stares straight at Darren, and Darren stares straight back. There's a long silence, and in it I can hear my own heartbeat; a quick, rushing pulse that fills my ears, seems to roar in the quiet.

"That right?" says Darren, calmly. He takes a cigarette from behind his ear and lights it. "How?"

"We don't know, exactly. Dropped somewhere in the panic. The fucking cops were chasing us."

Darren nods.

"Were they now? Did you not go back for it?"

"I'm not fucking stupid," replies Anto. "It'll be lying in the grass somewhere, or the cops found it, but either way, that's where it stays. If you want it, you go look for it yourself."

Darren keeps nodding, a slow metronomic bob, and with his thumb he repeatedly flicks the end of his cigarette, the ash dropping to the carpet. He looks at the gear on the table for a long time, then back at Anto.

"I don't believe you." He spits out the words.

My stomach lurches.

Anto smiles, but it's a more like a waxen grimace.

"I don't give a fuck what you believe, Darren. I know you make your money if just one of these gets through. We lost one. That's it. And it's your fucking fault we lost it."

Darren's head tilts to one side.

"And how's that, Anto?" he says.

"Because you fucking dickheads insist on delivering it to the wharves. It couldn't be any more bleeding obvious to the cops. And we're the fucking muppets turning up to get caught. You won't get another one through – not a chance; they're on to you. No more, Darren. You can find yourself someone else."

My head reels and spins. I feel like I'm ten pints deep. I want to vomit. If I walked right now I'd stumble. Anto is making it up as he goes along, and I have no idea what to do, how to act. Mercifully, Darren doesn't talk to me, or even look at me. He glares at Anto.

"You cheeky little fucker," he says slowly, and I hear the man behind us take a step forward. "You'll do what I fucking tell you to do, when I tell you to do it."

Anto says nothing, but I can see his jaw muscles clenching.

"You're getting nothing for this job. Not a fucking penny." says Darren. "And this is what you're going to do. You're going to go back home, like a good little delivery boy. Wait until you're contacted. Follow the instructions. Don't fuck it up. Understand?"

Anto says nothing, and Darren nods at the goon behind us, who steps forward and punches Anto in the kidneys. It makes a sound like a butcher throwing a carcass onto a concrete floor. Anto crumples and drops to the ground and lies there, wheezing and groaning. I'm frozen, rooted to the spot.

"Say 'yes, Merchant', you little fuck," Darren orders him.

Anto can barely make a sound, but he nods and his lips move.

"Yes. He said yes!" I blurt out, and Darren grins at me.

"Course he did," he says.

The Merchant nods at the man in the leather jacket, and he opens the door behind us, holding the gun casually in his hand.

I drag Anto to his feet and pull him towards the door. A stream of saliva slides out from the corner of his mouth and drips to the floor.

"Fuck," says the bouncer, and steps back. "Filthy little bastard."

I push Anto ahead of me and he manages to hold himself up. As we enter the hallway, I'm shitting myself that we're going to be shot in the back. I physically flinch when I hear Darren's voice again.

"Anto?"

We stop. Anto turns his head.

"If you lose another package, it will be the last thing you ever do."

I don't say a word to Anto until we're in the car and away. He managed to walk under his own steam once we got back out into the alleyway, but he was wincing and gasping with every step. I'm driving, and he reclines the passenger seat and lets out a moan.

"Be pissing blood for a while after that," he says. "Jaysus, he got me a good one."

"You fucking arsehole," I start, but he cuts me off.

"Listen, I know – I'm sorry," says Anto. "But you would never have agreed to it if I'd told you first."

"Agreed to what?" I bellow. "Agreed to what, Anto, you fuckwit?"

"We have to make another stop," he says, and he reaches around behind me, down under the driver's seat, grimacing in pain, and frees something jammed under there. He pulls it out and holds it up. It's the missing package.

"Oh fuck. Oh fuck, Anto. What have you done?" I say. I can't concentrate on the road, so I pull over. We're parked by the Liffey, and the rain is sweeping up the river towards us from the sea, a billion droplets picked out by the streetlights. The city suddenly seems deserted. I put my head in my hands.

"We're so fucked," I say.

"No we're not," he replies. "Calm down."

I know it's too late; there's nothing I can do to fix this. I'm in deeper than I could have believed possible, and all in under twenty-four hours; the blink of an eye.

Beside me, Anto checks his watch.

"We have to go," he says. "They're expecting me."

This time I don't ask Anto if I can come along. He tells me he's known the lads we're going to see now for years; he lived with them in the squat. A bit fucked-up, but sound men, is how he describes them – there'll be no bother. I don't argue with him. I sit in the car and watch him cross the road and disappear into the entrance of a Finglas tower block, and then reappear on the balcony of the fourth floor. Even from here I can see the bulge in his jacket from the package. He walks along balcony, looking back every few steps. He stops at a door, knocks, and is let in.

There's a surreal delirium to my thoughts; they skitter and slip like quicksilver. I try to think things through, to follow lines of thought to their logical conclusion, but they fracture and multiply and convolute until I'm back where I started.

Anto's in and out in under five minutes. He walks in front of the car, and the look on his face is pure lunatic, grinning while still grimacing from the pain. When he opens the passenger door, he tosses a brown paper bag into my lap.

"Done fucking deal," he says, leaning in. "Ever wondered what seventy grand in cash looks like?"

I can't take it any more. I open my door and vomit into the gutter. I retch again and again until there's nothing left in my stomach.

"Jaysus," says Anto. "What did you have for lunch?"

I don't reply, and he waits while I spit out the remnant into the gutter and then take a drink from a water bottle.

But Anto isn't finished yet.

"Come on," he says. "We've another stop to make."

I drive in a kind of daze through Dublin. He talks non-stop, but I'm barely listening, oblivious to all but his hand signals directing me where to go and the endless churn of my own thoughts.

After only five minutes or so Anto gets me to pull over outside a second-hand car dealership on the north side of the city, and he gets out without a word and goes inside. I sit there, watching him through the plate-glass window until he turns and beckons me in. I don't move until he comes back out again and opens my door.

"You don't want to miss this," he says, and wearily I follow him back inside.

One of the salesman stands up from his desk and ambles over. He's brushing crumbs from his trousers.

Anto looks at him and beams. He points at a black Jeep parked in the centre of the showroom. The price is emblazoned on its windscreen: thirty five thousand euro.

"We'll take it!" Anto shouts.

The deal's done in minutes. Anto waves a wad of cash in front of the salesman, and I think the man is going to call the cops there and then, but instead he takes it and puts it into the safe, fills out the ownership papers and hands Anto the keys.

Anto turns to me.

"See you back in Bundoran," he says.

I drive back in Shitty Shitty Bang Bang alone. By the time Anto pulls up in the Jeep outside my house that night he's towing a jetski, and lashed to its sides are three brand new surfboards – two big-wave guns and a tow board.

Chapter 12

"We can walk from here," insists Mikey, but Anto doesn't even hear him. He has singular focus. "Hold on you arseholes!" he shouts, and he floors it. The engine roars as the Jeep powers its way up the dune. But it's ridiculously steep, and the car slows and bogs. Sand fans up from the tyres and comes in the windows, scattering a fine layer over all of us. Anto gives the car no quarter. He works the steering wheel to the right and the Jeep crabs madly sideways and for an awful moment I think we're going to roll, but he straightens again and we resume our upward progress, inching our way to the top of the dune.

We've been driving down every coastal boreen for an hour because Mikey can't quite remember where this beach is, but he insists that the surf might be on, so here we are. I've been sending texts to Sinead; she spent last night at my place and we made up properly. I wanted to let her know about the cops, but I just couldn't bring myself to tell her. I'm gambling on the idea that if they get what they want, my purpose will have been served, and they'll leave me alone. I called the detective after the drop to the Merchant's, and told him everything I remembered about the place. He was pissed when I told him I didn't know when the next one was happening. I said nothing about Anto stealing the package and selling it to his mates.

"Go on, you motherfucker!" Anto screams, and when we reach the top the tyres suddenly bite and we lurch forward and nearly shoot down the other side. But Anto manages to brake in time and turns off the engine and we're suddenly there, looking over a pristine horseshoe bay.

"Oh fuck yeah," cries Anto, getting out of the car. "Oh yes!"

In the back, Mikey and Bren start whooping.

A left-hander breaks across the bay. It forms on the submerged reef at the southern arm of the bay, where square lumps of water rise out of the ocean, seemingly straight from the depths. Then, as it begins to break, a freakish mushrooming of whitewater blossoms up and avalanches down the face. It's a mess, but like magic it somehow reasserts order. It hauls itself upright and starts to spin along the reef. It grows, thins, becomes hollow, and breaks faster as it goes, the odd section holding the promise of a backdoor barrel. The wave gallops across nearly the entire bay, eventually expending itself almost on the shore below us – a full three hundred metres from the top of the point.

We're hypnotised by it, then there's a mad scramble for wetsuits. Anto climbs up onto a tyre, unties the straps and flings the boards from the roof racks down onto the sand. In minutes we're suited up and we sprint down the dune, hooting at each other. Anto ankle-taps Mikey and he goes down but somehow turns it into a forward roll and he's up again without missing a beat, his surfboard still tucked under his arm.

We tear down to the water's edge and run south along the sand until we reach the rocks where a rip runs like a conveyor belt out to sea. We only have to sit in it and it deposits us just fifty metres from the take-off spot. It's a playful size; four-to-five foot, and there's not a breath of wind. It's so good that I start to get the usual panic that the tide is going to fuck it up as soon as we get there.

Mikey is a paddling machine and he's first to the take-off, meeting an absolute jewel as soon as he gets there. The mushrooming swell gives him a little shunt and he's on his feet with his effortless style and then he's gone. I track the ridgeline of the back of the wave, but no flashing board appears, so I know he's racing, crouching, searching for the barrel. When he pulls off he's almost back where we started, and I see him raise both arms above his head. I hear him howl with delight.

There's no point in trying to outmanoeuvre Anto for the next one because when he's this frothed he'll just drop in. Bren and I give him the next one, and then Bren strokes into a cracker and is gone too. When his wave passes under me I see I've been rewarded; an even bigger wave rears behind it.

The take-off is easy; it's a languid gut-ride with all the time in the world to get to my feet. I weave a little on the open face, finding my groove. But the fatness quickly disappears. I can see the dark shadows of the rocks beneath the surface ahead of me and the wave responds to them, puffing up its chest, its shoulder lifting out of the ocean, the wall constructing itself. Suddenly I'm flying, and then pumping hard when a section rears well down the line. My focus narrows to a spot fifteen metres in front of me, and I rise up the face and set my line and I'm suddenly enclosed in the dark, oily cocoon of the wave. It's one of the sweetest barrel rides of my life; deep but wide open, ridiculously straightforward. The wave breaks uniformly, its folding lip rising and toppling, always just ahead. I relax, moulding my body into its almond aperture. I even have the presence of mind to slow myself, jamming my hand into the wall, and I'm thrilled by the sight of its opening receding away from me again. Bren must have been clipped by his wave because he suddenly comes into view ahead of me, watching me thread this tube, his hands raised. I hear him yelling at me and I blow out of the barrel just before I reach him and his smile is as wide as mine.

The rest of the wave passes as though in a dream. I get in a couple of turns but mostly it's a racetrack and I even backdoor another little section towards the end. I'm deposited in the shorebreak and when I get to the beach I can see Anto and Mikey running hard back around the bay. I pull off my leggie and do the same, hungry for more.

For the next two hours I see the rest of the boys at a distance or briefly in passing; like mismatched runners we're staggered at various stages of the circuit. The waves are so consistent that the wait at the take-off is rarely more than two or three minutes before we're off again, tearing down the line, searching for the tube.

I get spanked by the lip of a meaty one halfway down the line, but I don't care because I travelled so far back in the barrel for so long I felt like I'd never come out. When I regain my board I sit for a minute, and at the top of the point I see Mikey stroke into a cracker. He's so slight that the wave simply seems to collect him on its way past; he barely paddles and his timing is so flawless that he rarely has to scramble for a wave.

He's pure liquid as the wave gathers momentum and he weaves along the face, pumping for speed. I can see his bared teeth from here; he always looks like he's smiling when he concentrates. He leaves it so late to set his highline that the falling lip misses him by an inch, and then he's tucked in, relaxed, his arms hanging by his sides. He plays with the tube, toys with it; the roof skims his head, and he busts through a chunky chandelier without a wobble. It's a masterclass, and I simply sit and marvel at him until he scorches by me and disappears from view. I catch the following wave.

It's almost three hours later that I catch up with Anto at the take-off and he points out to sea: there's an ugly black line stretching across the horizon; a wind change.

"All she wrote, big man," he says. "What a fucking session, eh?"

I'm so tired I can barely lift my arms. On a normal day I'd have gone in long ago. On my last lap I passed Bren sitting on the beach, done in, a goofy smile plastered across his face. I realise I haven't thought of anything other than the next wave.

There's a rare lull, and Anto and I sit chatting like we're at the pub. All the manic energy has left him; drawn out of him by the ocean and exhaustion. It's the only time he ever gets quiet, when the hours in the sea have worked their cathartic magic. He told me once when we were walking home drunk from the nightclub that it's the best thing about surfing; the peace that he feels afterwards, the stillness of his mind. He said that it's like a veil gets lifted from his eyes; everything looks different. He feels order, can observe things as if from a distance. He thinks of his family, is overcome by love. He can make big decisions.

But it doesn't last, he told me. The noise returns, a building fizz in his head, crowding in from all sides, until he's consumed by it; driven by it.

Anto's prone to expressions of brotherhood in moments like this, and he doesn't let me down now.

"You're a good mate, Sam," he says, but he can't sit with the soppiness of it, so he adds: "for a sheep botherer." Then the next wave arrives, and he's gone.

My last wave is probably thirty seconds before the onshore arrives, and it's a little smaller, but it looks like it's made of blown glass. I stand tall on it and just cruise, and near the beach it slabs and I'm shot through a little backdoor tube right in front of the three boys on the beach and come out and simply step off onto the sand. They give me a round of applause, so I whirl my right hand in small circles in front of me and take a low bow.

We stand and watch the ocean and the onshore arrives as a solid thing, a wall of wind, and within a minute or two it's blowing ten knots, then twenty. Overhead a vast bridge of cloud arrives. The ocean has turned to ragged scrap before we even reach the Jeep, and we look out at it like the last audience members to leave after a concert, the show over, litter strewn across the stadium floor.

We pack up and get into the Jeep as the rain arrives, spattering the windscreen. Anto doesn't start the engine, but turns to Mikey and Bren in the back seat.

"Me and Sam have a favour to ask you boys," he says. I don't have a clue what he's on about, and I think he's about to crack a joke, but his face is serious.

"There's a pickup this Monday on Streedagh Beach. They're dropping them out to sea, and they're going to attach balloons to the packages so that they drift into the beach on the wind and we pick them up. All done at night. Easy peasy."

I stay quiet, a cold fear reaching into my chest, grabbing at my throat. No, no, no, my mind screams.

"Maybe the boys aren't into it," I say lamely.

Anto looks from Mikey to Bren, and when neither of them say anything, he drops the kicker.

"Three grand each," he says, a grin spreading across his face.

Chapter 13

It starts to rain just before dark; heavy droplets are conjured from the leaden sky and smack into us, driven by the gale.

"For fuck's sake," says Mikey as he, Bren, and Anto huddle together under the small tarp Anto has dragged out of the back of the Jeep. It's dirty and has holes in it and it flaps wildly in the wind. I'm the only one who has a waterproof jacket on.

The mood is tense, and I try to lift it – as much for my own sake as for anyone else's. Ten minutes ago I had to take some deep breaths to calm myself. I'm trying to act normal, but I keep looking around, imagining I see the dark shapes of people – of cops – up on the hillside. They know everything about this pickup; they visited me in the middle of the night again two days ago. They just smashed through the door again, same as last time, the fuckwits. I'm to make the pickup, then on the morning of the drop they're going to fit me with a wire. I tried to refuse, but they just laughed at me. I have no idea if they'll bust the Merchant this time, but they know it's a big shipment.

I yell to be heard over the wind.

"I have a question," I shout. "Why didn't you three dickheads bring raincoats? Like proper ones, with hoods and zips and shit? It's the same everywhere in this country. It never stops raining, and yet every single day I see people walking around without a raincoat. What the fuck is going on here?"

I mimic someone trudging along, depressed, head down. The lads watch me from under the tarp.

"In the name of science, let's examine what went through your little pea brains before you left the house this afternoon?" I say.

"You have to be optimistic," says Mikey.

"You do," agrees Bren. "Or else it might rain."

I can see the toothy grins of the three of them under the tarp.

"I reckon Australia – where it never rains – has more raincoats per capita than Ireland does," I say.

"More smug arseholes, too," says Bren.

"It's impossible not to feel superior to you three right now," I say.

We lapse back into silence. Anto hasn't said a word since we got here. Every two minutes he pulls out his phone and, shielding it from the rain, checks it although he knows there's nothing to check, then puts it back in his pocket.

I turn back to the sea and scan the horizon. Nothing. But the boat will be almost impossible to spot even if it's out there. Lines of whitewater stripe the ocean to perhaps half a kilometre offshore. The waves are huge; a proper Atlantic storm swell, and on the headland I can just make out the occasional puffs of white through the gloom as the waves hurl themselves against the cliff. The spray mists over us; I can taste the salt on my lips.

"Are you sure this is going to happen, Anto? It's fucking mental out there." Bren asks the question for all of us. Anto doesn't answer him and we're quiet again.

Twenty minutes pass. Now it's properly dark and I've started to shiver. The boys must be freezing and every now and again Bren reminds us of how shit the situation is. No one replies; there's no backing out now.

When Anto's phone pings it sends a jolt of electricity through me. I immediately feel sick again. I turn and watch him as he pulls it out of his pocket and it lights his face with a bluish glow under the tarp.

"Well?" I say.

"It's me ma," he replies.

"Ah, for fuck's sake," spits Bren.

"Only joking, ya muppets," says Anto. "It's them. Drop's been made."

Anto throws off the tarp, stands up and walks over to me. The two other boys greedily pull the extra canvas down over themselves.

"What do you reckon, Sam?" says Anto. "Twenty minutes?" There's fear in his voice.

"Fucked if I know," I reply, and the two of us stare out into the darkness. I'm trying to sound casual, but my heart's beating like a drum.

"I still can't believe they took my advice and canned the wharf pickups," he says.

"Yeah. It would be awful waiting in a nice warm car," I reply.

Anto laughs.

The rain pelts into our faces. I look at Anto and he smiles back, his teeth gleaming.

"Good to be alive, eh?" he says, and he throws an arm around my neck.

Twenty minutes later Mikey and I are at the south end of Streedagh Beach. Anto and Bren have walked to the north end and are working their way back to us. I can just see the pinpricks of light from their torches sweeping back and forth, disembodied and eerie.

The surf has churned the sea to foam, and piles of it emerge from the ocean and slide up the wet sand before the wind like ancient life forms crawling out of the primordial soup. When I lift my torch I see that the entire beach is stippled with this foam. It's going to make the job a whole lot harder.

Mikey and me begin to search; he sticks to the high-water mark and because the tide is receding I walk parallel to him but closer to the water. We zigzag our way along the beach. I stamp on the piles of scum and they disappear in a puff, the wind speeding the foam fragments away up the beach into the darkness.

We come together on a zag and I sense Mikey hesitating a bit so I flick my torch beam at him. His hoody is pulled up in a futile attempt at keeping out the rain, but I can still see his face. He looks like a frightened child.

"You all right?" I ask.

"Yeah," he says. "This is nuts, huh?"

I nod. "You having second thoughts?"

"Yeah… I think so," says Mikey. He shoves his hands into his pockets. "Anto's in deep. Maybe you too," he says.

"Ah… I don't know…" I say, but the lie is like concrete setting in my mouth.

"Sinead will be devastated if you get… if anything happens to you," he says.

I don't reply. I've been trying not to think about it.

Mikey turns away and resumes his search.

It's twenty minutes before we meet Anto and Bren in the middle of the beach, and they're empty-handed too.

"Fuck!" Anto bellows into the night sky.

For variety, we swap ends of the beach. Mikey and I keep heading north, while Anto and Bren go south. By the time we meet again another half an hour has passed. No one's found anything, and the boys are shaking with cold.

"What the fuck are we supposed to do now?" says Bren.

"Keep fucking looking, that's what," replies Anto. He's furious, agitated, as wild as the weather.

"Come on, Anto," whines Bren. "They're lost. They must be." He kicks at a piece of driftwood.

Anto's just about to unload on Bren when he spots Mikey's expression. He's looking out to sea, but only as far as the shallows, and peering hard in the darkness. He lifts his torch. The white slashes of the rain cut across the beam.

"What is that?" he says.

All four of us aim our torches. There's something floating in the spritzing foam.

Anto yells and starts to run, splashing through the water up to his knees. He grabs it and turns, a grin splitting his face. He's holding a yellow package about the size of a small paving slab, tightly bound with duct tape. A dozen black balloons are attached to it, bobbling about crazily in the wind. They look like the segments of an oversized blackberry.

"Yes! You fuckers!" he screams.

Anto wades ashore and we gather around him. He's looking down at the package cradled in his arms like it's a newborn baby.

"Fuck," says Mikey. "Shit."

"Fuck shit is right, Mikey boy," says Anto.

He pops the balloons one by one and the sound of them is strange out here in the wild darkness. He weighs the package in his hands.

"Fuck, this is a lot," he says. "This is so much."

Anto takes off his backpack and jams the package into it.

"Right," he says, looking up. "Where are the rest?"

It only takes fifteen minutes for the other packages to wash up on the beach. We find all twenty of them within two hundred metres of each other. Anto sprints up and down, leaping and yelling. His backpack is bulging, and mine is heavy on my spine. He stops for a moment as he passes me.

"We're in the money," he sings. He winks at me and runs off, disappearing into the darkness in the direction of the Jeep. My stomach is in knots.

Chapter 14

We trudge back along Streedagh Beach and up the dunes. When we get back to the Jeep, Anto opens the tailgate and upends the two packs so that the parcels tumble out into the boot. Bren, Mikey and I gather around and the four of us stand there in the pouring rain, staring at them in silence. They're still covered with the burst black balloons and they look like kelp-covered stones in the weak light of Anto's phone torch.

"Holy shit," he says quietly.

I peel off my jacket and the boys chuck their sodden jumpers and the tarp into the boot. We pile into the car, but with the heater on full it soon fogs up so badly Anto has to glue his face to the windscreen to see where he's going. Maybe they don't get rain like this in America because the Jeep's wipers are woefully inadequate; they slash back and forth but are no match for the deluge.

Out here, tracks run in all directions, but only some of them end up back at the road, and more of them lead to boggy swamps that even the Jeep won't be able to escape. Twice we have to reverse a long way back to a turnoff we missed or took by mistake.

I get a text from Sinead, but I don't answer it. No one speaks, partly in the futile hope that it will help Anto concentrate, but also because the gravity of what we've just done is well and truly sinking in.

Anto finally winds down his window to stick his head out into the downpour in case he can see any better that way. He can't. He stops the Jeep and announces that we'll have to stop here for the night. But he's messing; I spot the road up ahead, and I know we've made it.

"I'm singing in the rain!" Anto bellows out into the darkness, and his eyes are all but closed as the rain hammers into his face. He draws his head back in and turns to each of us, grinning, water streaming down his angular cheeks.

"We did it, boys," he says. "To the fucking pub, as fast as possible!"

Anto's clowning breaks not just the silence, but also the spell. Bren bangs on the ceiling of the car with his hand and hoots. I look over at Mikey, but the worry that's been etched into his face all evening has only lifted a little.

"You all right?" I ask him quietly. Inside I'm churning, far from all right, but I can't let it show.

He smiles weakly back at me.

"Yeah."

"Hi ho, Silver," yells Anto. He drops the clutch and sends gravel and mud flying as he turns the Jeep onto the road. The mood lifts by degrees the further away from the beach we get. Anto starts into one of his stories, telling us about the time he got into a fight at school and his mum had to go in for a meeting because Anto had downed the lad with a kick to the balls so vicious he had to go see a doctor and take a few days' rest at home. The headmaster and Anto's teacher had had enough of his shit, and were looking for an excuse to turf him out.

They called the meeting to make it official, but they hadn't reckoned on Anto's mum. She listened in silence until they were finished, then rose from her chair and delivered a fearsome speech, declaring that if Anto was thrown out of the school she would go to the Irish Sun with the story of the unfair persecution of her son at St Benedict's. She made up an elaborate tale on the spot, astonishing Anto as she recalled in great detail the days he'd supposedly come home crying, battered and bruised from repeated attacks by the school bullies. She made Anto hold out his arm and show them the scar from the cigarette burn one of them gave him, in reality an injury he got when he caught himself on a door latch as a kid. While Anto tells us the story, he jiggles around and puffs out his chest, transforming into his mum before our eyes. Then, like that, she's gone, and Anto's back in her place. He tells us that when they got back on the bus to go home afterwards he sat in beside his mum, looking at her with a newfound appreciation, until she turned to him and gave him a wallop across the head. He laughs so much the Jeep skews across the road.

Anto waves away my suggestion that maybe we should unload the gear first, and parks right outside the pub.

"Fuck that. I'm dying of thirst," he says, "and look at Bren – he's gonna fucking collapse if we don't get a pint into him soon."

We go in and there's only the two old regulars – Andy and Declan – drinking at the bar and two other men I don't know in one of the booths. Pat comes out from the back, and he laughs when he sees me.

"Ah jaysus, Sam, have you nowhere else to go on your night off?"

"I missed you," I reply.

Pat shakes his head, feigning disappointment.

"That's sad. Would you not have more fun spending time with that lovely girl of yours?"

Mikey and Bren laugh, but Anto's sometimes weird around Pat; he turns away and goes over to the fireplace. Pat goes back to Andy and Declan, who nod to me.

I go behind the bar and pour Guinness for Bren, Mikey and myself, and get a Powers and Coke for Anto. Anto has loaded so much turf into the fire we have to pull our stools back, but the heat feels good and my trousers start to dry out.

The Guinness goes down easy; I'm drinking fast and into my fourth when Pat comes over and says he's going home and asks me if I'll close up when we're done.

The men in the booth have gone, but the old boys at the bar are into a fresh one, so I tell Pat I'll look after them, too. I walk him out to his car. The rain has stopped and stars pepper the sky.

"Mind yourself, Sam," he says to me, his hand on the door to his car, but then he turns and looks at me for a long time and I wonder if he knows something, or at least suspects it. He nods slowly, thoughtfully.

"Mind yourself," he says again, and then he gets into his car, starts it up and lifts a finger to me as he drives away.

I stand there in the darkness for a moment watching his taillights, and I get a wave of homesickness. I feel adrift. I've squandered something, throwing my life away. Pat giving me responsibility for his pub has only made it worse. I suddenly want to chase after him, go home with him and pretend to be his son for a night, sleep in a bed with clean sheets, be fussed over in the morning by his wife.

When I go back inside, Anto's not there and Mikey says he went out to the Jeep. He's probably rolling a spliff. Mikey looks anxious again; Sinead says he has doe eyes, that they give away his emotions, and they're wide and worried now. I sit down with the boys and Bren says they have to tell me something.

"We're not going to do it again," he says.

"The beach," adds Mikey, as if I don't know what he's talking about. But I've been waiting for it.

"It's too risky. We live here," says Bren.

We all live here, but I know exactly what he means: that they're from here. The two of them search my face, looking for a reaction.

Relief floods through me, but I try not to show it.

"To be honest, I'm surprised you agreed to it in the first place," I say.

"Three fucking grand each is why," says Bren.

"But we don't want that now, either," adds Mikey quickly.

I nod, and glance towards the front door.

"Did you tell Anto?" I ask.

"No," says Mikey, looking down at the table. He flips a coaster.

"Will you tell him for us tomorrow?" asks Bren.

Up at the bar, Andy knocks on the wood with his glass and I get up to serve them. I see Anto come back in to the pub while I'm looking after the old boys, but he goes straight past Bren and Mikey and into the toilets.

There's a bit of banter with Andy and Declan because the Aussies have just lost to the Irish Gaelic football team in the International Rules. I tell them that it's because their round balls bounce funny and because the poor Aussies were confused by the wet stuff falling out of the sky on top of them, and frozen stiff.

By the time I sit back down with the boys, Anto's back and I can see something's different right away. He's got a crazy grin plastered across his face and his eyes are huge.

"In the jacks," he says. "Right-hand cubicle, top of the cistern." He nods like a maniac.

My blood runs cold.

"You fucking didn't?" I say.

"What?" he replies. Defiance is Anto's default whenever he's challenged. He sticks out his chin at me. Wha?

I get up and walk to the toilets. Inside I see Anto has pulled the cubicle door closed and when I open it I immediately see them: three long stripes of white across the yellowing plastic of the cistern. I stand and stare at them, disbelieving. I feel like going back out there and yelling at Anto, but there's the old men at the bar. It's too fucking late, now, anyway.

I pace back and forth for a while, rubbing my face in my hands, trying to think. The door swings open and for a moment I freak out, thinking it's Andy or Declan, but it's Anto and he's holding out a rolled-up twenty.

"You'll need this," he giggles.

"Anto, you fucking arsehole…" I start, but he throws an arm around my neck and pulls me close.

"Relax," he says. "The Merchant won't know. He won't have a fucking clue. I can tape up the package, good as new. None the fucking wiser. Anyway, I told you he has huge losses built into his business plan."

He touches the side of his nose, and does a little tap dance on the floor.

"Oh fuck it's good," he says, and he prances his way back into the cubicle and hoovers up a whole line.

"Sorry about that, Mikey," he says, but then I see him go for the pocket of his jeans and I notice the white blooms of the coke spilled down his trouser leg. He digs his hand deep into his pocket and pulls out a fistful more which he dumps onto the cistern.

"Just in your fucking pocket, is it?" I say, shaking my head at him.

"Your turn, cobber," he replies. "Chuck another shrimp on the barbie, mate." He grins like a lunatic.

I'm suddenly gripped by Anto's fatalism, his madness. I'm in deep and there's no way out. He's infectious and I long to forget. He holds out the rolled-up note for me to take and he boots me up the arse as I walk into the cubicle.

"Go on, you little fucking beauty," he says and stands behind me watching as I snort half a line up each nostril. In seconds I feel it; like ice-cold water running through my brain. It cuts through the Guinness like sun clearing fog.

Anto puts his head back out through the dunny door and calls in Bren and Mikey. God knows what old Andy and Declan think we're doing, but it seems I no longer give a shit.

Bren's straight into it, but Mikey says he doesn't know if he will. Then he sees that I've had a go, and lines up behind Bren and the two of them are out again in no time rubbing the powder off their noses and grinning like eejits. Anto grabs us all around the necks and draws us into a little huddle there in front of the urinal.

"Look at you, you beautiful bastards," he says, and we all stare back at him. His eyes blaze as he turns to each of us, nodding and smiling. I think he's about to say something profound and we all wait for it, but then he says it feels like the top of his head is going to pop off and he giggles like a little kid. He gives Mikey a kiss on the lips and lunges for Bren but Bren bats him away and the scrum disintegrates.

"Yesss, boys!" Anto yells. "We fucking did it!" And he starts dancing again. Reaching into his pocket, he grabs another handful of coke and flings it into the air, then lifts his face up to the descending cloud of powder and sniffs at it as it drifts down and settles in his hair and on his shoulders.

I stick my head out the toilet door, but Andy and Declan have gone and the pub is empty. I lock the front door and this time we cut up the lines on the bar. Anto bellows for tequila and I find a dusty bottle at the back of the shelf and we polish it off in less than half an hour. I pour four more Guinness, and into shot glasses go four Powers chasers. We've cranked up Pat's transistor radio as loud as it can go, which isn't loud at all, and it blares out the country music station he likes to listen to. Dolly Parton's 'Jolene' is playing, and somehow it's the right music, and we're singing our hearts out to it.

I get another text from Sinead, but I don't read it.

By midnight, we've crossed into madness, and we stagger out onto the street.

"To the nightclub," yells Bren, but then we remember that it's a Monday. Anto stands on the pavement, skinning up a spliff, ranting about what a shithole Bundoran is, but Bren suddenly speaks.

"Lads! Lads!"

He urges us all to be quiet, and looks to the sky.

He sticks a finger in his mouth and then holds it up theatrically. He has our attention.

"The wind's gone offshore," he says. "Mullaghmore will be on in the morning."

Chapter 15

Chunks of vomit drop into my outstretched hands and slip through my fingers, spattering into the water. I look down at it, as though I need to examine it to figure out what's happening. There are pieces of what looks like half-digested meat and I remember that when I got home last night I ate three cold sausages from the fridge.

"You fucking animal," shouts Anto, and when I look up at him he's grinning at me. He turns and paddles further up the point.

The stupidity – both mine and Anto's – of coming out here, into huge, heaving Mullaghmore, hungover, is fully apparent to me now. When he knocked on my window this morning with his stupid 'Here's Johnny' routine, I'd been shitting myself. But I saw the jetski behind the Jeep I had some hope that we might zoom around a bit and just watch from the channel, but Anto was having none of it. He was going to paddle it come hell or high water.

I retch again and again, gasping for breath and spitting lumps down my wetsuit until nothing remains in my guts. I give silent, desperate thanks that there's a lull in the waves because if I'd been caught inside while I spewed I would have been fucked.

When it stops, I immediately feel better, but my throat thickens again when I see the black ridges of the next set rising in the distance like a Himalayan mountain range. I lie down and paddle, staying wide, playing it safe.

Anto does the opposite. He doesn't hesitate for a second, paddling deeper into the take-off zone, head down.

I get out a little further, and stop again when I know I'm well out in the channel. I suck in lungfuls of air, tasting the sour sting in the back of my throat. I wash out my mouth with seawater but it doesn't help; it just burns even more.

The first wave of the set is a broad, mid-sized hump, and it moves well over the reef before it breaks, avalanching down the face without truly barrelling. It almost looks like fun; as least it's relatively user-friendly for Mullaghmore. As I crest it, I see Anto already stroking for the second one. It's a different beast entirely; the water draws back off the reef, going below sea level, and the sea surface is suddenly pockmarked with boils. The wave is shades darker than its predecessor. Its bulk rears like the muscular shoulder of a giant.

Anto's right on the peak, perfectly positioned. I can't believe he's going for it. He strokes hard, flattened to his board. Then he's sliding, and he springs to his feet, but for a few moments the illusion has him travelling backwards, up the face. The wave gathers itself and launches skyward, towering above him; three times overhead, four. Anto looks like a stick man – like a classroom doodle drawn on an exercise book – a study in charcoal, dwarfed by the cartoonishly big wave at his back. His arms are thrown high and outwards like wings as he plunges into the drop. It's sickeningly fast. He's just a fraction off-balance, and he skitters out onto the flats for a split second too long before he's able to regather for a bottom turn. As I go over the shoulder I see that he's lost; the lip strikes behind him and explodes, eclipsing him with its blinding speed and awful mass. He disappears in the eruption of whitewater and spume.

There's another wave coming, but I'm well out in the channel so I turn and watch for him, searching for his black hood in the seething mat of white foam left in the wake of the wave. But he doesn't appear before the next wave steams past, and I physically flinch when I feel the power of it and see the jets of water forcing themselves through the back of it as it breaks.

Ten more seconds go by and I'm starting to freak when I see his board surface and start to tombstone. I can't believe that it's still attached to him, and then I wonder if his leggie is wrapped around a rock. But Anto suddenly pops up and I see him gasping for breath as he pulls himself onto his board. I crest the next wave and lose sight of him again. It's the last wave in the set, and it's smaller but it must clean him up awfully, breaking right in front of him. Again, I watch helplessly as he takes an age to appear in the maelstrom. But up he comes. He's struggling, I can see, and I paddle in towards him as fast as I can.

The three waves have dragged him two hundred metres down the reef. By the time I reach him, he's out in the channel, lying flat on his board, his head resting on his hands.

"Anto!" I yell. My voice cracks with worry. "Anto! You OK?"

He doesn't look up.

"Your turn," is all he can manage.

"This is fucking nuts," I say.

Anto doesn't reply for a while. He sucks in lungfuls of air and when he finally lifts his head I see a rivulet of blood coming from his nostril.

"You're bleeding," I tell him.

"I'm baptised," he replies, snorting out blood and snot. "A two-wave hold-down."

"Yeah. Congratulations," I say.

Anto sits up on his board.

"Go again, I reckon," he says.

"You'll lose your board," I say. "What happens then?"

"Dunno. Let's find out," he says.

I say nothing to that, and the two of us take the long paddle back to the top of the point in silence. I stop again at the edge of the channel, but Anto doesn't hesitate; he paddles straight back to the take-off zone.

"You coming?" he yells over his shoulder, but I can't reply. I can already see the next set approaching, and I know that I don't want any part of it. I feel the fear and shame rise up inside me. I sit up on my board and watch from the channel.

Again, Anto lets the first wave go, and paddles deep for the second. It's a carbon copy of his last wave, brutal and black-hearted. He barely even looks at it, but commits to the paddle immediately, and this time he's even deeper. He scrambles to his feet and the drop is insane, bottomless, but somehow he hangs on. I've never seen anyone progress like Anto; six years ago he'd never held a surfboard under his arm. His learning is instinctive, his muscle memory constantly refining itself. He's already adjusted his attack; he doesn't straight-line the drop, but angles and knifes hard and pulls up. Instantly, he's enclosed by a barrel with a lip as thick as a car. He's about to be swallowed whole. I picture an orca coming out of the depths to attack a seal, its jaws gaping wide.

Anto doesn't try to pull through the back, doesn't bail. He stands tall, spreads his arms wide and looks right at me. Just before he's lost from view, I see him get skittled in the most brutal way. He's travelling at warp speed, but the wave is breaking so fast it's as though he's being sucked backwards into the awful tunnel. He's flicked off his board by the foam ball and I see him go down on his guts, skid once, twice, before he's dragged up the face to the ceiling of the barrel. Then he's lost in the raging water as the wave collapses in on itself.

I'm suddenly furious with him; I see that his psychopathic death wish is going to end with me trying to pull his body ashore through the rocks. My fear and worry channels itself into useless anger.

But this time Anto pops up quickly, and he's on his board and racing for the channel. He takes the tail end of another wave on the head but he's relatively unscathed and when he paddles back out to me he's grinning like a madman.

"You gotta get some of that!" he shouts, laughing. "That's some fucking buzz, boy."

Anto sets off again for the top of the point, paddling fast. He's on fire, in his element, loving every minute of it. He's not even thinking about me. His focus is absolute.

That day, Anto caught two more waves. His last one was a vicious wipeout, another over-the-falls horror show, and afterwards when he pulled on his legrope his board had gone. We never found it.

But his second-to-last wave is etched into my memory. This time, he waited for it, playing cat-and-mouse with the monstrous sets sweeping through the lineup. The swell angle wasn't quite right, I realised; most waves were unmakeable – simply breaking too fast. But when he saw the one he wanted, he didn't hesitate.

The creeping dread I felt as I sat on my board, watching him, evaporated as he stroked into it. There was something in his timing. He rose early, dropped forever. His bottom turn was lazy, smooth. He didn't pump, just set his line, stood tall and looked up as the herculean lip blotted out the sky above him. The sun had emerged again and lit the scene with an emerald hue. It was the biggest wave I'd ever seen, the best barrel ride I could imagine. He was locked in from beginning to end; ten seconds of glory the likes of which I knew now that I would never experience. I was sitting in the channel well down the reef, and had a grandstand view of the entire wave. By the time Anto pulled off, planing across the flat water, he was only metres from me. He said nothing, didn't even look at me. He just turned and paddled back out.

We don't speak much on the drive back to town, and when Anto drops me off he looks straight ahead.

"I'll pick you up this afternoon, big man," he says. "One o'clock." And then he's gone.

I walk down the lane to my house. The shed door is open, and I throw my board clean through it. It clatters across the concrete floor.

Chapter 16

I stand in the shower until the hot water runs out. My hangover is now a dull hum in the back of my head, but I'm anxious, still shaken from the Mullaghmore surf, and jittery from the coke. The nausea has been replaced with a gnawing apprehension about this afternoon.

I have to eat, and I have to see Sinead, so it's the café for breakfast.

Against the odds, the weak sun has prevailed and the sky is clear of clouds. The air is cold and clean. It feels good to walk. I welcome any distraction; any respite from my thoughts.

When I reach the main road I get a look at the ocean. The swell has dropped a lot, like the power has been switched off. But it's still huge, and the Peak – straight out from Bundoran – looks all-time, with eight-to-ten-foot bombs rising up out of the ocean and folding themselves over with the precision and symmetry of closing envelopes. There's only half a dozen people out and part of me wants to turn around and go home and suit up and paddle out to prove to myself that I can still handle solid surf.

I'm halfway down the hill when I see Mikey and Bren walk out across the road in front of me, boards under their arms. They spot me and wait. Bren looks like shit.

"Well," says Mikey cheerfully. "How's the head? Ye mad fuckers didn't go to Mullaghmore this morning, did ye?"

I nod.

"Bullshit!" says Bren.

"We did. Anto got some bombs. I was too chicken."

"Don't blame ya, man. I'm shitting myself going out here," says Bren.

Mikey smiles at me. He tilts his head at the ocean.

"You coming?"

"Nah," I say. "I have to go see your sister. I'm trying to come up with a legitimate reason as to why I didn't reply to any of her texts last night."

"Good luck with that," he says. "Send in the explosives team first."

"How are you feeling, Bren?" I ask. He looks wretched.

"I'm fucking rough, man. Anto wouldn't go home." says Bren. "This fucker here's peachy. Look at the big healthy head on him." Somehow Mikey's done it again; he has a reputation for surviving big nights unscathed.

We chat a few minutes more, then go our separate ways. Down the road a bit, I hear Bren call my name. I turn.

"Last night I let Anto know that Mikey and me aren't going to do it again. You're off the hook."

Relief washes over me. I want to hug them both, but instead I just nod. I wish I could do the same.

"How did he take it?" I ask.

"Better than expected. He didn't say anything," says Bren.

I can almost see the weight lifted from Mikey's shoulders.

The two boys turn and jog down the road. I watch them for a while, chatting to each other and laughing, and I get an image of them as little kids, groms heading out for a surf together. I envy them for their easy relationship, their families, their place in this community.

The café's busy when I get there and I stand in the queue waiting to order. Sinead's in and out of the kitchen but when she sees me she comes over and gives me a sneaky pinch on the arse on her way past to clear a table.

"Sit down and I'll come to you," she says, and there's a spot near the window so I grab a newspaper and head for it.

It's a few minutes before she can get to me and I read a story in the paper about some gangland killings in Dublin. The cop quoted in the article says there's a feud going on over drug supply and it freaks me out so much I close the paper again. Nausea rises in the back of my throat every time I think about this afternoon.

I jump when Sinead comes up behind me and slides her arm around my waist. She glances back at Gillian, her boss, to make sure she isn't looking, then kisses me.

"You missed out last night. I wanted to do very bad things to you," she says, her eyes widening. She looks beautiful; wisps of hair have escaped her ponytail and frame her face. I'm glad she's forgiven me, but there's a rock in my stomach.

"And I opted to spend the night in the company of three men," I reply. "I blew it, huh?"

"Foolish boy. Where were you?" she asks. There's a sharpish edge to her tone.

"Pints at work. Anto, Bren, and your brother. Ended up being kind of a big one."

She shakes her head.

"Saddos," she says.

Sinead doesn't ask if I got her texts. She goes back into the kitchen and comes out with a full Irish breakfast – sausages, rashers, black and white pudding, eggs and mushrooms – but I can't eat much of it. I'm sick with nerves. She sits with me for a minute. She's acting a bit weird; looking into my eyes a moment too long like she's trying to figure out what I haven't told her, but she says nothing.

By the time I've picked over the fry, Sinead has a half-hour break and she wants to go back to her flat for something. We walk past the shuttered amusement parlours and shops for lease. It's a depressing part of town until you emerge onto the seafront where the houses gather themselves around the rocky shoreline. Bundoran epitomises the proverbial 'faded grandeur' – an old lady with torn stockings and smeared makeup, gin on her breath, but still able to flash a winning smile. Sinead hates it, but even more so in the winter. She says it's closed for business, but I caught the tail end of the holidaymakers and I couldn't stand it. They'd stream out of the holiday park and down into the town to get drunk in the pubs while their kids hung out in the amusement parlours and smoked sneaky fags in the alleys. Then they'd all troop back up the hill home again, not once going near the beach.

I start to tell Sinead about Anto's wave this morning, but her eyes harden and I tail off. She has no time for Anto any more.

When we get to her flat I go to put the kettle on, but Sinead has other ideas. She comes up behind me, reaches her arms around my waist and starts to unbutton my trousers. I spin around and she smiles at me, her eyes flashing wide.

"I've got ten minutes," she says.

Despite myself, I'm turned on. Distracted. Theatrically, I suck the breath in between my teeth.

"Dunno. Could be tight."

"Bullshit," she replies, laughing. "I'll probably have time for a shower and a cup of tea afterwards."

She kisses me, hard and urgent, and her hands slide down my boxers and my nerves evaporate, replaced by an urgent desire, fuelled by the adrenaline of last night and this morning. I crave release. I suddenly can't get enough of her, can't get close enough, deep enough. We fuck right there in the kitchen, her perched on the edge of the bench. It's over in minutes but we both come, and our breathing is light and quick and fills the space afterwards. Her arms are around my neck, her head on my chest, and she hugs me for a long time, saying nothing. Then she looks up at me with her beautiful eyes, and kisses me. I feel a stab of fear, a fluttering of nerves.

"You know what?" she says.

"What?"

"I think I love you." She doesn't wait for an answer, but turns away from me and walks to the loo. "You might as well make that tea!" she calls out as she goes.

When we leave Sinead's flat we go our separate ways. I've told her Anto and I are going surfing again while the swell's still firing. She's twenty steps away from me when I call her name. She stops and turns. She smiles, her teeth flashing, her gorgeous eyes liquid.

"I think I love you too," I say, my heart in my mouth.

She looks at me thoughtfully, her head cocked to one side.

"Correct answer," she says, and winks. She turns and continues, then gives a little hop and clicks her heels together. She doesn't look back. I grin like an idiot.

I get to the address I've been instructed to go to by the cops five minutes early, but they see me through the window and let me inside straight away. There are three of them; the two that came to my house and another, who has his back to me. When he turns it takes a few seconds for me to recognise him – it's Sinead's cop friend from the nightclub – Finbar. He averts his eyes, concentrating instead on the equipment in his hands: the wire.

I'm told to strip off my shirt, and they work in silence, taping it to my chest. They tell me to get dressed again and they test it. I have to push a button to activate it, but I'm not to push it until I'm close to the Merchant's or the battery won't last. Then I'm done. They let me out and I walk home, and on the way I decide that I'm going to tell Anto everything in the car on the way to Dublin, and we can decide what to do together. If he agrees to help the cops then maybe they'll go easy on us. I'll call the detective on the way and tell him.

I've got twenty minutes before Anto is due to pick me up so when I spot the Jeep parked on the road outside my house a pulse of apprehension sears through me. I pull out my phone to double-check in case I'm late, but I'm on time; Anto's early.

As I get closer, I see that the Jeep's empty; Anto is nowhere to be seen. I look up and down the street but it's quiet; no people, no cars. I pick up my pace, and when I reach the Jeep I look inside. It's empty. I mean, really empty. Gone are the cans and wrappers in the footwells, the plastic buckets and wetties and spare leggies in the back. Anto has cleaned it. The coke is gone, too.

I've almost reached the house when I realise something else: the Fiat wasn't parked out on the street. I run back out to make sure. I haven't driven it in almost a week, and I try to remember if it was there this morning when Anto and I left for Mullaghmore. But there's nothing except the dust and leaf litter that had collected around the tyres and marks where it should be.

I go back to the Jeep and try the handle, but it's locked, and I stand there in the street trying to think. It dawns on me that Anto has swapped the Jeep for my crappy car so he doesn't attract attention during the drop this afternoon. I'm suddenly angry; it's typical of Anto, and I fume, thinking of what I'll say to him when I see him. I figure he must have gone to the shop for something. I walk back down the lane to my flat and go inside and sit in the armchair, staring at the door, waiting for him. I call him but he doesn't pick up and his stupid answer message irritates me intensely.

One o'clock comes and goes and I can't squash the little panicky sensation that begins to prickle my scalp. I stand and put the kettle on, but I don't make tea. I tell myself that he's just chatting to someone in the street, he'll be here any minute, and it occurs to me that I should bring a jacket so I go into my room. It's then that I see the package on my bed – a regular bubble-wrap job from An Post, with my name scrawled across it in Anto's handwriting.

I pick it up and it's heavy and something slides around inside. My hands are shaking as I tear it open, and two things fall out and land on the bed: the keys to the Jeep, and a gun – a pistol.

Fear rips through me and I have to sit down, but my impulse is to get away from the gun and I get up again and walk back out into the kitchen, sucking in deep breaths and blowing them out hard again. I walk around in circles, struggling to think, to assign reason to whatever the fuck is going on. After a few minutes I go back into my bedroom, pick up the gun and put it back into the envelope. I bury it under the socks in my dresser. Then I take it out again and pull the table under the hatch into the attic. Climbing onto it, I open the hatch and put the gun carefully down on one of the rafters. It's only when I get the hatch closed again that I begin to calm down and think more clearly.

It's half past one; it's obvious that Anto isn't going to pick me up – he's gone already. He either knows about the cops, or is trying to protect me, or both. Then a thought hits me like a hammer between the eyes, and suddenly I know what he's doing, where he's going.

I grab my phone and the keys to the Jeep and rush out, slamming the door behind me and going at a sprint down the lane. The Jeep roars to life and I floor it, a loud squeal from the tyres ripping through the neighbourhood, but I know I'm probably fucked already, that I'll never get there in time to stop Anto.

The Jeep climbs out of Bundoran, and I dangerously overtake a few locals tootling along in their cars on the quiet streets, seeing them look over at me in alarm. Then I'm clear of the town limits and on the open road and I put my foot down, driving as fast as I dare.

It's only when I reach the motorway that I pull out my phone and make the call.

"It's me," I say. "Anto left without me."

There's a pause. Then the detective's thick North Dublin accent fills the space, rage-filled, clipped. "You useless little fucking prick. You'd better not be trying to help him because I will have you in a cell so fast your feet won't touch the ground, understand? How long ago did he leave?"

"How the fuck should I know?" I say.

I can sense him thinking, calculating. "Keep your phone on," he says. Then he hangs up.

Chapter 17

I push the Jeep to its limits and make it to the outskirts of Dublin in under two hours. Again and again I try to call Anto, but it goes straight to voicemail and eventually I give up.

Just as I'm coming off the motorway my phone rings. The detective's voice is strained, furious.

"Where the fuck is he? He should be here by now."

"Maybe he stopped for a piss," I reply. "He'll be there – just sit tight."

He starts to say something else but I hang up. My hands are shaking, and I grip the steering wheel as tightly as I can to make them stop.

I drive like a madman through the streets, trying to remember how to get to the tower block where Anto sold the stolen gear to his old flatmates, hoping like fuck that I'm right. I screech sideways into a main street and straightaway I spot the second-hand car dealership where Anto bought the Jeep. I can't help but laugh out loud; a bitter cough of a laugh.

But the dealership gives me a landmark, and now I know where I am.

Two minutes later, I pull up three streets away from the tower block. I walk the rest of the way. I remember which apartment it was; fourth floor, fifth door along. I repeat the location over and over to myself, in time with my footsteps; a nervous mantra.

When I get there I stand and watch from the corner for a few minutes. I spot the Fiat parked on the other side of the street. Anto is nowhere to be seen. Outside the tower, two young boys are kicking a flat football around, keeping up a running commentary as they play. They stop and stare at me as I approach. Strewn all around on the threadbare grass are empty cans and bottles, cigarette butts and fast-food wrappers.

The stairwell of the tower block scares the shit out of me. Every single light has been smashed, and the steps are covered with rubbish and reek of piss. There's a gang of boys on the first landing, bombed out of their heads. They stick their legs out as I pass, trying to trip me up.

"Here, what's the password?" one slurs. I keep my mouth shut and push past his leg, holding my breath, but they just laugh and stay put, too wasted to care. On the next landing a lone man stands sentinel in the corner, his hood pulled over his head. He doesn't move or make a sound.

I pass him and bolt up the steps, two at a time, until I reach the fourth floor. I'm breathing hard as I walk along the balcony, searching for the right door.

Standing outside it, I'm crippled by indecision. I'm know I'm a rat in a trap, cursed two ways. I raise my fist to knock, but just then I hear a shout in the street below. It's one of the young footballers.

Leaning over the railing, I see two cops running across the road, and three more coming along the pavement on this side. They're the armed response unit, dressed all in black, each carrying a rifle. One of them stops, and looks up. I recoil, pulling back from the edge. But I know that he saw me.

I turn and hammer on the door, yelling Anto's name.

Chapter 18

When Anto opens the door he's well freaked out to see me. I can see three lads behind him, back in the lounge; all wearing tracksuits and with shaven heads. They look like children, frightened and panicking. They've all got guns, which they're pointing at the front door, at me. Behind them I can see the parcels of gear piled up on a coffee table. I can even see the one with the hole in it; Anto never even bothered to reseal it.

"What the fuck?" hisses Anto, and he tries to drag me inside. "Get in here."

I resist. "The cops are coming," I tell him. "They're downstairs."

He goes pale.

"Oh fuck," he says, and he sprints back into the lounge and returns with his black backpack. It's bulging. In the room behind him I can see the three boys frantically grabbing the parcels; and that's all I see because Anto pulls the front door shut and takes off along the balcony, slinging the bag over his shoulders as he goes. I follow him.

We reach the corner of the building and carry on. The balcony continues along this side, too, but Anto stops and climbs over the balustrade. He begins to lower himself until his legs are dangling in space. He looks at me.

"Can't very well take the fucking stairs, can we?" he says.

Once we're over the side we have to lower ourselves hand over hand down the thin vertical supports between the concrete slabs that make up the balustrades. My heart's in my mouth as I edge down, and my knuckles are crushed and skinned because the space is too tight for my hands. I can only just reach the banister on the floor below with my toes, and don't know how I'm going to let go, but Anto has already made it and he grabs me and pulls me in. Footsteps seem to be coming from everywhere, and I can't tell if it's the cops chasing us, or kids running from the cops. One of the lads from the landing sprints past us, wild-eyed and unsteady on his feet.

"This way," says Anto, and unexpectedly he runs back towards the stairwell.

"They're coming from that way," I hiss, but he ignores me, and there's fuck all else I can do but follow him.

Anto halts before we enter the stairwell and this time he climbs over the balustrade on the building side of the balcony. There's a space there, and it forms a kind of chimney, with walls on three sides. He braces a foot on each side – one outstretched, and the other hard up under his arse – and starts to lower himself. When I look over the edge my heart stops. It's three floors straight down. The chimney is smooth and featureless.

"Fuck," I say, and Anto looks up.

"Hope you put your good trainers on this morning," he jokes grimly. "Come on, piece of piss."

I can hear men running along the balcony above me, but I also hear heavy footfalls on the stairs, very close now. I know I could stay right there, and meet them; send them along the balcony to give Anto a bit more time. But I also know I'm screwed; there'll be no mercy for me this time, so I climb over the balustrade and, hanging onto it by my fingertips, try to position my legs like Anto's. I push against the wall, testing the grip of my shoes. I paste them onto the concrete. Slowly, I put all my weight onto them, and it takes every bit of my courage to let go of the balustrade. I then sit, paralysed by fear, a storey above Anto, and fifteen metres above the ground. If I slip I'll kill us both.

I can't bring myself to move; to shuffle downwards, but I'm below the level of the balustrade and when the cop goes past on the balcony he doesn't see me. The road is obscured by the side of the building, but I hear cars pull up, doors slam. If just one cop walks around the corner we'll be seen straightaway.

I look between my legs. Anto is flying down now, foot, foot, hand, hand. I watch him for a few seconds, and then try it myself. I'm sick with fear. My hands are shaking and my legs feel too weak to bear my weight. But I manage a sequence, and I shuffle down half a metre. I do it again. My feet don't slip, but I'm pushing them so hard against the walls that I'm quickly exhausting myself. I realise I have to relax, or I won't make it to the bottom. Easing off a tiny bit, my grip is still firm, and I descend a few more metres, and then all of a sudden I get the rhythm and start making good pace down the wall. Anto has reached the ground, and in fairness to him he waits for me when he could just as easily bolt. A minute later, I'm beside him. My heart pounds so hard and so much adrenaline has flooded my body that I shake all over.

Anto peers around the edge of the building.

"Fucking hell," he says. "We're popular."

I don't want to see. We run the other way without looking back, and cross the road and go down an alley which comes out on a high street. Anto goes into a pub. There's maybe a dozen people inside and we walk the length of the place, down past the bar and the toilets and into the beer garden. Through a gate at the back there's an exit into the street behind. When we come out of that there's a graveyard across the road so we cross over and go in and Anto slows to a walk. He doesn't turn around, says nothing to me.

The tombstones are so old they've almost weathered down to blank stone, the inscriptions worn away from two hundred years of Irish wind and rain. Only a few remain upright; most tilt at crazy angles or have given up completely and lie flat on the ground. It's quiet and still as we pick our way through the graves. No sirens or car engines can be heard.

"Anto," I say.

He turns, looks at me.

"Have you got nothing to say?" I ask. My anger is rising again.

"You tell me, Sam," he replies. He juts out his chin. "Why don't you call your detective friend?"

My stomach flips. I gape, like a goldfish. Anto starts walking again, but I run forward and grab him and spin him around.

"How do you know?" I ask.

Anto smiles, but his eyes are hard.

"How the fuck do you think? I got a call from the Merchant. You think he hasn't got cops on his payroll? The merchant knows everything. Your fucking girlfriend told her cop mate. She wanted him to just pop around to your place and give you a scare so that you'd stop, but he went and told the fucking drug squad."

My head spins. I can't speak. I look at the ground.

"Yeah," says Anto. "Now he's figuring it out. When did the cops get you?"

I swallow, trying to find my voice.

"They came to my house after Teelin Wharf," I reply.

"Thought so," said Anto. He spits on the ground.

"What are we going to do?" I ask lamely.

Anto laughs.

"We? We aren't going to do anything. You're on your own, me old cobber. You just helped me, so now you're as screwed as I am. If I was you, I'd fuck off back to Australia as soon as humanly possible. It's either the cops or the Merchant that'll get you – take your fucking pick. You can have some of this if you want it." He jerks a thumb at his backpack. I shake my head. The thought of the money makes me sick.

Anto keeps walking, and I follow him dumbly. I'm so lost in thought that I don't register the whine of car engines and the screech of tyres back at the entrance to the graveyard.

"How the fuck…" says Anto, and it's only when he starts to run that I realise they've tracked us down. Together we vault the fence onto the footpath. I look back and see four cops have run into the graveyard after us, but when they spot us they turn and run back to the cars. They'll have to go around the block. Anto sprints towards the main street, but I hesitate. A realisation hits me: along with the wire I'm wearing a GPS tracker. I reach up under my shirt and rip it off my chest. I throw it as far as I can, back into the graveyard. Then I turn and run up the road, in the opposite direction from Anto. Crossing over, I jump a low wall and sprint through one yard and then over the hedge at the back into someone else's. I keep going. A dog gives chase but I'm gone over the fence before it reaches me. I cross another road and run behind a row of shops. I come to a bridge, slide down the bank and splash along the stream bed up to my knees for ten minutes, the freezing water numbing my feet and overhanging blackberry bushes scratching at my face. Ahead, I spot a train station and as I scramble up the bank and go over the bridge I can see there's a Luas due in three minutes. I sit and wait, shaking, until it pulls up. It's bound for the city centre. I board the train and it's only when the doors close that I begin to breathe normally again. The people on the train look at my sopping shoes and trousers and move a few seats away.

As the Luas gathers speed, I'm hit by a thought so visceral and awful it feels like a blow.

Sinead.

The Merchant knows everything.

I clutch at my pocket. My phone is gone. It must have fallen out of my pocket somewhere. But the Jeep keys are still there.

I push the button for the next stop. The train pulls in. The doors seem to take an age to open. Finally they slide apart and I push out and break into a run.

Chapter 19

I find my way back to the Jeep without seeing any cops, and drive it back to Bundoran even faster than I drove it to Dublin. I have to stop for gas but it's the only stop I make and I just about burst waiting in line to pay. I buy a cheap mobile phone because I think I can remember Sinead's number but after getting it wrong a few times I give up. I try the café because sometimes the staff have an after-work drink there, but nobody answers. I fling the phone into the passenger footwell in disgust and stand on the accelerator even harder.

I have to go to my house first, and I freak when I see the front door ajar. I force myself to creep around the outside, looking through the windows, but it's useless – it's pitch dark. I have to go in.

The door swings open without a sound and I reach around and switch on the light with my heart in my mouth. When I step inside I'm so fucking scared I can hardly breathe but it's silent and empty and I exhale heavily. Climbing on the table, I open the attic hatch and feel around the rafters until my fingers touch the padded envelope.

I leave the gun inside it; I don't want to look at the thing. Leaving the house, I don't bother to close the door. When I get to the Jeep, I toss the envelope onto the passenger seat.

Parking the Jeep on a street parallel to Sinead's, I go at a jog around the block. The envelope is tucked under my arm, and it feels like a lead weight. My pulse races just carrying it.

Stopping on the other side of the road, I crouch between two parked cars and watch Sinead's house. Her front door is closed. There's a light on in the front room – Sinead's bedroom – but the curtains have been pulled across the window.

I have a key for her house, and I turn it over and over in my hand. There's no one on the street, so I rise and run across the road and, as quietly as I can, push it into the lock. With my other hand I reach into the envelope and close my fingers around the pistol, but I don't pull it out. Everything feels like a dream; time slows, sounds are muffled and indistinct, colours are hazy.

As slowly and quietly as I can, I turn the key. It rotates smoothly, and there's only the faintest of clicks as the lock releases and the door swings inwards. Immediately I hear the TV, and the place is warm, and I start to relax and breathe again. I close the door behind me. I go down the hall and I'm just about to call out Sinead's name when I hear a cough – a man's cough. Instantly, a jet of adrenaline crackles through me.

I'm almost at the door of the lounge, and need only to lean forward slightly to see inside. The big armchair has been moved over in front of the gas fire, which is lit and on high. Over the top of the chair, I can see a man's head. He wears a baseball cap, and is watching a gameshow on the TV, mumbling and nodding to himself. I can see his hands, the tattooed fingers curled over one of the chair arms, a packet of cigarettes in the other. I fight a powerful urge to turn and run.

I move slightly and more of the room comes into view. There's someone stretched out on the couch, covered by the chequered blanket that Sinead keeps in the lounge. I move a little more, and

I'm surprised to see that the blanket is pulled up over the person's head. I'm confused; unsure of what I'm looking at. Then I see the strand of long blonde hair twisting out from under the blanket.

The realisation that I'm looking at Sinead makes me gasp; a quiet, involuntary inhalation of breath. It's a physical spasm, a sensation like being plunged into an icy lake, or being electrocuted.

As if in slow motion, the man in the chair turns around. I notice strange things: the teardrop tattooed under his eye, the stud in his ear. There's an expression of mild surprise on his face, like he's just recognised someone at the pub.

I pull the gun from the envelope and for a few seconds I just point it at him and we're locked in a silent standoff. Then I tilt the barrel up and ram the butt into his face. It takes him by surprise; he doesn't even recoil. I hit him so hard that he falls off the armchair onto the carpet and the back of his head cracks hard off the hearth of the fireplace. He doesn't make a sound. Then I'm astride him, and I drive the butt of the revolver down on his head over and over until he stops moving, and I keep hitting him for a while after that. Part of his skull has collapsed; there's a grotesque crater in his head. There's not much blood at first, but then it starts to pool and seep from the injuries I've inflicted. I drop the gun and reel backwards off him, horrified, and stagger to my feet.

I go to Sinead and sit down on the edge of the couch. I'm frozen, afraid of what I'll find when I pull down the blanket. The gameshow blares in the background. I take the corners of the blanket and peel it back slowly, with infinite care. Her face is perfect, peaceful, beautiful. Her eyes are closed, and for a moment my heart leaps with hope, but then my fingers brush her skin and it's dense and cold. Somewhere under this blanket is the injury that killed her, but I don't want to see it. I play a trick instead. I stare at her face and tell myself that she's asleep, waiting for me to slide under the blanket with her, to wrap myself around her. For a moment the delusion works, but then I bend down to kiss her and the lifeless chill of her lips brings me back to reality and I recoil away and stand up and feel a hysteria, a madness, rise up inside me. It's like my head is going to split open.

I don't know how long I've been here in the lounge. Reality crumbles and distorts, and I'm swaying and staggering under the weight of it all. But I'm suddenly back in my body, and men are banging on the door, shouting through the letter slot.

"Billy, you fucking muppet!" says one of them. "The bleedin' chips are getting cold."

I'm on autopilot as I pick up the gun and walk back down the hallway towards the front door. I'm without thought, stunned. I stand at the door for a moment, but instead of opening it I go into Sinead's room and close the door behind me. There's a crack in the curtain, and I peer through it. There are two of them outside. I recognise the huge guy in the leather jacket from the Merchant's, but not the other one – he has a skinhead and wears a white tracksuit and he looks wiry and mental. He's furious. He orders the goon to kick in the door. The brute hands him a newsprint-wrapped parcel and takes a step back.

Suddenly, I'm thinking more clearly. I make a decision. Reaching between the curtains, I wait until his foot crashes into the door before I unlatch the window. They don't hear it. The goon doesn't break the lock the first time, and when he kicks it again I push the window open a crack.

"That's it, you got it. Put your shoulder to it," says the tracksuit. "Fucking Billy. He's probably taking a dump, the filthy little prick."

There's a splintering sound as the timber around the lock shatters and I push the window open wide, and draw back the curtain and put a foot up on the sill. When I hear them come into the hallway I pull myself up into the window frame and squat for a moment on the sill. I should be jumping, sprinting away, but I hesitate. I'm overcome with horror and fear. I'm abandoning Sinead to these animals, and I'm disgusted by the cold voice of reason in my head that says there's nothing I can do for her now. I'm a guilty traitor, but too much of a coward to do anything about it.

I look at the gun in my hand and I realise that I have no idea if it's even loaded. I tuck it down the back of my jeans.

When I jump out, my shoulder glances off the window frame and I watch in horror as it swings around. There's a loud clunk as it reaches the end of its hinges. The sound sends a jolt through me, and I straighten up and run. I charge out of the gate and turn right and sprint along the footpath, and I'm almost at the end of the block when I turn to look back.

I see the indicator lights on the car parked outside Sinead's house flash twice, illuminating the two men racing to open its doors.

Chapter 20

I hear the whine of their engine, the squeal of tyres. There's no way I'll make it to the Jeep before they come around the corner, so instead I cut down a driveway and run along in the streetlight shadow by the side of a house. The driveway ends at a garage and I'm hemmed in on both sides by the house and a high fence. There's a wheelie bin against the wall and all I can do is crouch down behind it. I feel like I'm in a kids' cartoon where the big dumb monster hides behind something so small that he sticks out on all sides.

It's only seconds before they turn into the street, and there's the awful hiss of tyres as they drift sideways across the tarmac. The car rips past the end of the driveway, its engine roaring, and the streetlights pick out the skinhead hunched over the wheel. I can just make out the hulking dark form in the passenger side. They speed down the street, past me, past the Jeep, and turn right at the end.

I'm suddenly aware of the pistol digging hard into my back as I squat, and when I pull it out I stare at it like a madman.

There's a smear of blood on the handle. It sickens me, and suddenly feel a desperate urgency to be rid of it. It's a fucking stupid thing to do, but I open the lid of the wheelie bin and drop it inside. I don't even wipe my fingerprints from the handle.

I feel like I'm wading through waist-deep water as I run to the Jeep; my legs are leaden and weak, and it seems to take an age to get there. I'm overwhelmed by the fear that, any second now, they'll realise their mistake and come blazing back around the corner.

My hands shake violently as I jam the keys into the ignition. I want to sit quietly, to close my eyes, to process what's happened. My head cycles between the fear I'm feeling and the horror of what I've witnessed. I keep seeing Sinead's hair curling out from under the blanket, remembering the hard, cold feel of her skin. A shudder goes through me, an involuntary spasm that brings a wave of nausea into my throat.

I start the Jeep and pull out onto the road. I have no idea where I'm going to go. I do a U-turn and head in the opposite direction from them, but there are only two ways out of Sinead's estate and they both lead back to the main road. There's a possibility that they'll go around the block first, that they'll come back this way, but I don't know what else to do.

When I reach the main street there isn't a car to be seen in either direction. I turn right and head north; my instinct is to keep clear of the Dublin road. I crave safety, comfort. I want to curl up into a ball.

I try not to speed as I drive through the town, but there's a feverish panic in me pushing down on the accelerator, and I have to fight it. A car appears from a side street and my heart thumps wildly, but with relief I realise it's not them. Another appears in my rear vision, but pulls over outside the chipper. I start to breathe again.

I'm only two hundred metres from being able to turn off and continue north on a back road when I see their car. It crests the rise and comes down the main street towards me so fast I have no time to do anything. I can't U-turn, and there's nowhere to pull off into a driveway or side street.

I'm wearing a baseball cap, and all I can do is pull it down over my eyes. I have no idea if they'll recognise the Jeep, if they even know that it's Anto's car.

Seconds later, I find out.

They scream by me, and I dare not look as they pass. The next thing I hear is the shriek of brakes and the ripping sound of their tyres biting into the concrete as they handbrake turn in the road.

I'm unthinking, going on pure instinct, as I stamp on the accelerator. The Jeep charges away, and in seconds I'm going eighty, then a hundred along the narrow main street. I glance in my rear-view mirror and I can see they're coming after me, but already I've got some distance on them. But I just know the skinhead is going to drive like a maniac.

Up ahead, on the right, is the pub. There's a stooped figure outside, bending down. As I get closer, I see it's Pat. He must hear me coming, because he stands up suddenly and turns. I can't help myself; I'm compelled to look at him, to see a friendly face. He holds a brush in one hand and a dustpan in the other, the broken glass in it glittering in the streetlights. When he recognises the car, and sees me behind the wheel, his expression turns to shock; his eyes wide, his mouth open. He glances down the street, at them, and then back at me.

Then I'm gone and speeding away and I turn right into a street which I know has a narrow lane that connects to a parallel road. If I can turn into that before they reach me I might be able to lose them. I keep my foot flat to the floor until I'm too scared to go any faster.

I reach the lane and fly into it as fast as I dare, the Jeep's tyres scudding sideways and then suddenly gripping. It's unlit, and I pray there's no one here. The headlights show a clear path aside from the wheelie bins studded all along one side. But just before I reach the other end, the headlights of their car suddenly light up the inside of mine, and I pound the steering wheel in anger and frustration.

Out of the laneway, I wrench the steering wheel to the right and for a moment I think I'm going to roll the Jeep, but it releases and slides instead, and I have to fight to stop the fishtailing overcorrections I make. I'm slamming the gearstick around, and I jam it into second as I reach the main road again. It screams in protest. There's a car coming past, and I almost drive straight out into it and cry out in fright and relief when I manage to stop short.

This time I turn left, heading south. I hurtle down the hill, past the seafront and up the other side. Someone crossing the street has to run to get out of the way. Then I'm out of the town and on the open road.

The look on Pat's face stays with me, and I'm struck with a desperate horror. I've fucked everything up; it's all my fault. The tears stream down my face as I speed into the night, into the deep black of the countryside.

The road is thankfully clear of cars, because I'm right on the edge of control. I round corners and the Jeep drifts into the other lane as I try to keep up as much speed as I can. I can see their headlights behind me – perhaps three or four hundred metres back. When I reach the roundabout at the junction of the N15 there are other cars on the roundabout, so I turn off my headlights in the desperate hope they'll confuse the ones of the cars going north with mine. But it's no good; there are so many streetlights blazing on the roundabout they could see me from a mile away and in my rear-view I watch them come after me. I switch on the headlights again and plant it.

I suddenly think of a new plan: get to Sligo and drive straight to the police station. Perhaps I'll smash into it to get their attention. It's a twenty five-minute drive on a good day, and for about three minutes I'm hopeful, but I realise that they're gaining on me. I almost drive off the road twice looking in the rear-view to keep track of them, and the Jeep's wheels pound over potholes on the hard shoulder before I can wrestle it back on the road.

They catch me at Grange. The Jeep is powerful, but whatever they're driving is quicker on the open road, or at least they're willing to push it harder. I come into the town doing over a hundred, but the skinhead is going even faster. He drives straight into the back of the Jeep so fast that my head slams back into the headrest, then jerks forward again, and the Jeep weaves right across into the oncoming lane. I miss a parked car by centimetres.

I get shunted forward, and instinctively brake, but in the rear-view I see them coming to ram me again.

There's a side road to my left and I floor it and haul on the wheel and the Jeep whines in protest as it rounds the corner. They follow, but they have to turn more sharply than I did, and they lose control; their car slides and spins almost a hundred and eighty degrees. In seconds I've put fifty metres on them, and by the time I see their headlights maintaining a steady beam again I've bought myself some time. I glance in the rear-view and see them, and behind them there's another set of headlights, further back. It's probably a local, but I can't help but think the worst: that they've called reinforcements, and now there are more of them.

The road I'm on is narrow; the average one-lane Irish country road, and I pray that no one is coming the other way. But the road is clear and quiet. A kilometre along it there's a hairpin bend, and they've gained on me again. Just as I begin the turn I see the flick of light. The bullet hits the Jeep like a hammer striking a piece of roofing iron and moments later I hear the crack of the shot. It scares me so much that I involuntarily jerk the wheel to one side and come close to losing it.

I push the accelerator hard to the floor when I get through the other side of the turn, leaving them behind a little bit, and that gives me an idea. A hundred metres further on I come to an intersection, and instead of blazing straight through I turn left and floor it again. They drop back a little further; their car can't match the Jeep for acceleration. I need to keep turning.

I turn left and right on every lane I see, and there's a mad lattice of them through this part of the countryside. Bit by bit I'm leaving them behind. I now have no idea where I am, but it doesn't matter; if I can keep doing this, eventually I'll lose them. After each turn it takes longer for their headlights to appear. The second set of headlights I don't see again.

Now I've got some breathing space I begin to think more clearly. I realise that if they catch me again, I'll go off-road; I'll smash through a fence and drive into a paddock. There's no way they'll be able to follow me in their car. I can't believe I didn't think of that earlier.

There's a hard left-hand turn up ahead, and I pull out wide before the corner, wait until the last second to brake, then pull in close to go around it. I floor it halfway around. I'm going way too fast, and the wheels bite for a second and the Jeep pulls away, but then suddenly I'm adrift, travelling sideways across the road. I should keep the accelerator floored, but I'm shocked by the movement and I do the complete opposite; I hit the brake. The back of the Jeep immediately swings wider, then grips, and suddenly I feel the left side of the car rise off the ground. I swing the wheel back to the right, thinking I might be able to plough through the hedgerow, but it's too late. I'm pressed into the driver's door as the Jeep begins to roll. It feels slow at first, ponderous, but once the car reaches its apex it happens in a blur of speed. The windows all explode at once, and I feel a brutal force against my right arm as the door crumples and collapses in on me. Then I'm upside down and thrown to the left and back upright as the Jeep rolls over and over with astonishing velocity. For a moment the car is airborne, spinning, before there's the huge impact of it hitting the ground again. It seems to go on forever; my body helplessly rag-dolling under the awful forces in the rotating violence.

At some point, my head strikes something hard and unyielding, either the column forward of the driver's window, or the collapsing roof of the Jeep, I don't know which. But the impact knocks me out cold.

Chapter 21

I'm woken by a searing pain across my chest. I claw at it, gasping for breath, and the tang of petrol fumes fills my nose. I'm upside down, and my neck is bent right over by the collapsed roof of the Jeep. I grope at my hip with my left hand, and my fingers are slippery, wet with something viscous and warm. Finally, I locate the seatbelt buckle and manage to release it. The pressure comes off my chest and the relief is instant. For a moment I slump there, but I'm still upside down and now all my weight is on my neck.

There's a narrow slot of maybe twenty centimetres where the window used to be, and I inch towards it by crabbing along on my shoulder. I have to turn my head sideways to get it through but as soon as I do I can twist my body and take my weight on my back and there's enough room to get my legs down onto the ceiling of the Jeep.

I lie there, breathing heavily with the effort. Above, the sky is clear and moonlit and filled with stars. It's freezing cold.

I strain to listen. I can hear the ticks and creaks of the car settling, cooling, and there's a low hiss, too, coming from somewhere inside the engine bay. But that's all. I can't hear their engine.

When I turn my head I can just make out the hedgerow in the moonlight. There should be a gaping hole where the Jeep passed through, but strangely it appears to be intact. I remember the weightless, airborne moments when the Jeep left the ground and realise it must have flown over the hedge.

I have no idea how long I've been out, but I'm filled with the black dread that the men are walking silently through the grass, right now, approaching the wreck of the Jeep, their pistols raised. I curse myself for leaving the gun back in the wheelie bin.

I can feel the broken glass in the window frame cutting into my back through my sweatshirt as I wriggle out, but there's little I can do about it. I get my arms out of the window and try to grab the door handle to hold myself up off the glass, but it doesn't do much good. The sticky stuff on my hand is blood, but there's little pain from it, and it's too dark to see how bad it is. The smell of petrol is stronger now; it stings my nostrils, burns my eyes.

I'm halfway out of the window when I hear the puff of a flame igniting in the engine bay. It's an innocent little sound, unthreatening – like a gas hob sparking or the pilot flame igniting in Sinead's lounge-room fire.

At the same moment, I hear something else: the distant sound of a car being driven hard, the gear changes being left too late. I realise they must have driven right past, and now they're coming back.

Pulling my heels up under my arse onto the ceiling of the Jeep, I shunt backwards. The pain of the glass digging into my back is forgotten. With two big thrusts I'm through to my hips, and one more and I can sit up.

There's a *whomp* from the engine bay, and a tendril of bright orange fire snakes out from a space left between the Jeep's buckled bonnet and front side panel.

I scramble to my feet and run. The ground is boggy and uneven, cut up by the cattle walking over it, and I stumble and fall down twice. I'm driven by pure panic; that at any moment I'm going to be mown down by the explosion and a billowing wall of fire. Behind me, I can hear the skinhead's car, close now. I don't turn around.

When the Jeep explodes there's a flick of white light like a camera flash. Then the shockwave and the heat and the noise come all at once with a violence that throws me to the ground. I sprawl in the mud and cover my head with my hands and lie there until the sound of the explosion rolls away into the night.

When I turn, the Jeep is engulfed in flames five metres high. The fire burns so fiercely I can feel the heat from where I lie. It's so bright I also nearly miss the flash of headlights further down the field through the steel gate. They flare for a second, then flick off, and then I can see nothing. But I know it's them, and I turn and run.

The ground rises, and when I'm far enough away from the glare of the fire I can see that before me is a huge, dark mass, blotting out the stars. I look up and see the craggy outline of dozens of peaks, and suddenly I realise where I am: at the base of Ben Bulben mountain.

I'm on an exposed slope, so I bolt for a line of trees a hundred metres further up on the hillside, scrambling up over sheep tracks and slipping in the mud. But, before I reach them, there's a *thwip* in the mud in front of me and to the side, and when milliseconds later I hear the sound of the gunshot, I know I'm fucked; they've seen me. I hear one of them shouting angrily to the other as I make the trees and in their shadow I run sideways along behind them. When I get to the end of the row, I look out across the fields from my heightened vantage point, but there isn't a farmhouse to be seen.

I consider hiding here; lying down and covering myself with dirt and branches for camouflage, but it's a stupid idea; I know they'll find me if they come up the hill. I have to skirt around the low branches to get a clear view back to the orange glow of the burning Jeep, and it takes a moment to spot them. They've split up, and both are walking towards the trees. The flames behind them distort their shadows into ghoulish giants on the hillside.

The skinhead is at the far end of the row of trees, but the big one is no more than a hundred metres away from me. I turn and run, upwards, towards the summit.

Chapter 22

My breathing is laboured and thick and my tongue hurts. I'm scrambling uphill through rocky outcrops and low scrub and gorse, and I'm covered in mud from falling over so many times. Where the sheep and cattle have walked the grass is threadbare, and it's slippery as fuck underfoot. My hand has started to throb, but it's so covered in blood that I can't tell where the actual cut is.

There are ridges and crests in the hillside, and so far this has kept me hidden from the men chasing me, but I know that they're still there and following me because I hear them shout out to each other occasionally. They're still spaced well apart, combing the hill as they climb.

The slope steepens, and funnels upwards into a kind of chute between two rock flutings, and I have to use my hands to keep going. I hope like fuck that there's a way through the chute; that it won't end at a cliff I can't climb. I've seen Ben Bulben from a distance, and I know that if I take the wrong way there's no possible route up; just bare limestone cliffs. But it's impossible to tell in the dark. The moon is bright, but it only serves to deepen the shadows. I suddenly come upon a sheep, startling it, and it gives a terrified bleat and gallops away downhill. I almost yell in fright.

I get higher. I'm relieved to see that the chute doesn't end; that I can get up through it, but it's hard going. I have to force my way through dense gorse and tall thistles and I grunt with the pain of it. Finally, I make it to the top of the chute, and over the little rise at the top.

Immediately I can see my mistake. Over to the right of the chute, beyond the fluting, the slope is even and clear, and I immediately spot the man at the base of it. I squint in the gloom. It's the skinhead. He hasn't seen me yet, and I watch him for a moment. He's fast. Faster than me. He has his head down, and he's digging deep, climbing hard. I consider turning around and going back down through the chute, but I have no idea where the other man is. I might end up right down on top of him.

I turn again and go, running uphill for as long as I can, until I physically can't keep it up any more and have to slow to a walk. Even then, I don't look back. Sweat drips from my forehead, and my heart beats furiously in my temples.

I've climbed for maybe twenty minutes, and it takes me by surprise when I realise I'm at the top of the mountain. It levels out quickly, and then there's nothing but its signature tabletop spread out before me. It's pearl-hued in the moonlight and beautiful, but all I see is its featureless expanse. There's nowhere to hide.

I start running, heading for the other end, thinking that maybe I'll find another way down, but in seconds I'm fucked because I run into bog and sink up to my knees. It doesn't make sense; a swamp on top of a mountain. The freezing water seeps into my trainers, and the mud sucks at them, threatening to pull them off. I keep going, hoping to come out the other side, but the bog only gets deeper.

I've haven't gone far when the skinhead calls out to me.

"Oi!" he shouts, and it stops me in my tracks. I wait for the shot to ring out, for the awful impact between my shoulder blades, but there's no sound other than my own ragged breathing. I turn. He's standing at the edge of the bog no more than fifty metres away, his gun raised. In the moonlight I see him grin.

"Get over here before I put a fucking bullet in your back," he says. He doesn't even have to shout; the night is so still that it sounds like he's whispering it in my ear.

Chapter 23

The skinhead stands on the edge of the bog, waiting for me. He doesn't speak while he waits. The only sound is the mud and water sucking at my feet, and the rasp of my own breathing: a shallow hyperventilation. The world lurches and sways.

When I reach him, he's breathing heavily too. White vapour ghosts from his mouth into the air, like the breath of a dragon.

"Closer. Stand still," he orders. I can do nothing; his raised gun is pointing at my chest. I do as he says until I'm three feet away, facing him.

He stares at me, and I think he's going to shoot me, right there and then; that the sick fuck wants to see the look in my eyes when he pulls the trigger. Instead, he rams the gun into my face, and I feel one of my teeth shatter as the barrel smashes into my chin and rides upwards, tearing my lips. The blow sends my head backwards, and I reel and fall into the mud. I stay there, holding my mouth as the blood starts to pour from it.

"Get up," he orders. I hesitate for a moment, and he screams at me.

"Stand up you fucking prick!"

I stagger to my feet, and he bats my hand away so he can see my torn lips. Blood drools down the front of my top.

"Move," he says, and indicates down the mountainside with the barrel of his gun.

A third of the way back, we meet the other man. He's bent double, wheezing, trying to recover from his exertions. When he sees me, he straightens, and smiles at the skinhead.

"Fair play," he says. "You caught the little bastard. Bring him here and I'll give him a fucking clatter."

I'm rigid with fear, stripped to my lizard brain, my base instinct for survival the only functioning part of my cognition.

"Yeah, yeah," says the skinhead. "Let's get off this stupid fucking hill."

We slither and slip down the mountainside. The big man falls twice, and he only gets angrier as we descend. In the gloom, the skinhead points me in the wrong direction, and we have to turn and go back up again before we can go down the right way.

Finally, we reach the row of trees near the base of the mountain, and I think about making a run for it, but they close up beside me, perhaps sensing my thoughts. I know I won't get five metres before they drop me with a bullet. They stop and wait silently, listening for sounds from below.

I peer down at the field through the gaps in the tree trunks. I can see the Jeep – a hulking dark shadow. Smoke spirals up from it into the air, but the flames have gone out. No one has seen the fire, no one has come.

Satisfied, the skinhead tells me to get moving again, and we walk down the slope to their car.

"Do it here?" says the big man.

"Good as any," replies the skinhead. "We we won't be interrupted, that's for sure." He nods at the smoking Jeep.

"If no one heard that, they won't hear this prick scream."

Ice bolts through my veins, and freezes my limbs.

The big man opens the boot of their car and pulls out a red plastic jerry can.

"First," he says to me as he walks over, "you're going to pay for making me run up that fucking hill. And then you're going to tell us where we can find your pal Anto."

Chapter 24

The big man punches me in the face so hard it feels like a sledgehammer. I'm flattened, and my head whiplashes into the ground. There's a white flash across my eyes, and my vision mists at the edges, then slowly clears again. I turn onto my side and try to curl up, but he puts his boot on my shoulder and forces me onto my back again. My face – all around my right eye – hums and pulses from the blow. But I blink, and realise I can still see out of it.

"Holy shit," marvels the skinhead. "Conor bleedin' MacGregor, what?"

In the time it has taken for me to regain my senses, the goon has uncapped the jerry can, and now he upends it on me. The air is immediately thick with the ferocious bite of petrol fumes, stinging my eyes and throat. He pours it up and down my body, and it soaks through my clothes. I scrabble backwards, but he simply follows me as I move. He keeps going until the can's empty, then steps back.

"You stupid fucking prick," says the skinhead. "Ye got greedy, didn't you, you and that fucking rat pal of yours?"

He pulls a Zippo lighter from his pocket.

"Now. Down to fucking business," he says. "Where's Anto?"

From somewhere deep inside me comes a boiling anger, a paroxysm of rage. It rises through me like bile.

I spit, blood mixed with my saliva.

"Fuck you," I say.

He kicks me in the ribs, and then stomps twice more in the same spot. Pain lances through my body.

"There's a part of me that hoped you'd hold out on me," he says. "At least for a little while, anyway."

He flicks open the lid of the Zippo.

"Your missus got lippy too, you know that?" he continues. "Stupid fucking bitch bit my hand."

He squats down beside me, tilts his head.

"You know what? I feel genuinely sorry for you, man. What sort of a fucking slag grasses her own boyfriend up to the cops? Granted, she was a ride, but what the fuck was she at? The way I see it, I've done you a huge fucking favour by offing the cow. Ruin your fucking life, a missus like that."

The big man grunts with amusement.

The flint wheel rasps on the Zippo. A flame springs up, and the skinhead's emaciated face is suddenly lit with the dancing light.

"Where is Anto?" he says slowly.

I'm adrift, loose from my moorings. Gone are the cold ground, the mud, the petrol fumes. Gone is the pain in my ribs, the throb in my eye socket. I'm pure, white rage; raw, elemental.

"Go fuck yourself," I say.

The skinhead stands and takes a step back.

"Last chance," he says, and he cocks his wrist, poised to throw the Zippo at me.

I close my eyes. I don't want his face to be the last thing I see. I conjure Sinead; her beautiful eyes, her wide mouth, her soft lips.

I can suddenly hear her voice; she's whispering my name.

The sound of a gun rips the night apart. I jerk violently on the ground as though the shot has struck me, and then again when the sound comes a second time. I curl into a ball. My eyes are open, but I'm unseeing, senseless, catatonic.

The gun's report rolls away across the mountainside like thunder. Still I don't move. The squelch of mud. Pressure on my shoulder. A squeeze. I turn finally, emerging from my cocoon.

Pat is kneeling beside me in the muck.

Chapter 25

Pat helps me to my feet. He's gentle and unhurried and his voice is calm, authoritative.

"Come on, up now," he says, and he holds my elbow until I'm steady. I'm disorientated, and my ears continue to whine from the sound of the shotgun.

Pat has broken the gun and it sits in the crook of his arm as though he's a farmer returned from shooting pheasants. But behind him, the two black shapes of the men lie in the mud. I can't help but stare at them, and I think I see one of them, the big one, move slightly, but it's hard to tell.

"Don't worry about them," says Pat. "Come with me."

He guides me back to the gate where their car is parked, opens the door and feels in the ignition. When he finds nothing, he walks back over to the bodies, leaving me standing there. I've started to shiver uncontrollably, rippling spasms travelling up and down my body.

Pat is back and I hear the jingle of car keys.

"Get in," he says, and I do what he says. I'm like a child waiting to be given instructions. I can't think for myself; something is broken, malfunctioning.

Once I'm sitting in the car, Pat pulls out the seatbelt, reaches around me and plugs it in. He jams the keys into the ignition.

"Listen to me, Sam," he says. "You're to leave Bundoran, right away. And you're to leave Ireland."

Pat gestures back towards the field, to the bodies of the men lying out there in the frozen darkness. They've become ghosts, or zombies; somehow more frightening than they were alive. I picture them rushing back through the hedgerow, like ghouls, their feet dragging across the earth.

"There'll be more of their gang looking for you tomorrow morning, and you'd better be gone."

I stare straight ahead, out into the blackness. The outline of the mountain is marked by the line where the stars disappear. It's an inky blot, an absence of anything.

"Look at me," says Pat, and I turn to him.

"Keep your wits about you, boy. Don't worry about them – I'll look after everything here. You just get away as fast as you can. Go on now."

But I still don't turn the key in the ignition. I don't deserve to get away, to leave behind all the shit I've caused. Pat doesn't know about Sinead, and if he did he might have left me at the mercy of the men.

"I… I'm sorry," I say to him, and he reaches in and touches my head, gently, like a father would a son.

"Be careful," he says. "Drive normally, slowly, and take the back roads if you can once it gets light." He takes his wallet out of his pocket, pulls out some notes and presses them into my hand.

"Now off with you," he says. "Go."

I start the car. As I back out, the headlights swing across Pat, and he looks so old and tired and I can't believe I'm leaving him there. But he waves and smiles as though it's nothing, like he's farewelling a visitor after a cup of tea. As I drive away up the road, he fades into blackness in the rear-view mirror and I can't help it; I start to cry uncontrollably. Great sobs heave up from my belly, and tears spill down my cheeks.

Chapter 26

I'm a mess most of the way back to Bundoran, but I start to think more clearly when I get to the outskirts of town. The urge to go to Sinead's house is powerful; the idea nags at me that she might not actually be dead at all, that in fact I've left her to die, but the memory of the rubbery chill of her skin comes back to me like a sledgehammer blow.

I know what I have to do. I need to go to my house, get my stuff, and leave – forever. I drive slowly past it and park around the corner on the next street. There's nobody around, and I have no idea what time it is; the clock in the skinhead's car is all fucked up. I walk back to the laneway, and staying in the streetlight shadow created by the fence line, I make my way slowly to the house. The door is open, just as I left it. Silently, I stand inside the doorway and listen, not moving. I stay that way for a full minute, before switching on the light.

The house is empty and freezing cold. I get a torch from the kitchen drawer and flick the lights off again.

I strip off, leaving my muddy, petrol-soaked clothes in a heap on the floor. In the torchlight I can see blotchy red burns from the petrol all over my body, and when I get into the shower they sting a bit under the hot water. The water blushes pink with the blood from my hand.

I wash furiously, soaping myself all over as quickly as I can, and driving my fingernails through my hair. When I turn off the water I get an awful feeling someone is outside the bathroom door, waiting for me. Like a fucking idiot I jump out, my right fist drawn back, but there's no one there.

I can see now that the cut on my hand isn't deep. I dry it with a towel and wrap a bandage around it.

There's a clothes horse in the lounge and I take a T-shirt, jumper, jeans and socks from it and pull them on. I left a pair of trainers by the couch and I force my feet into them without undoing the laces. I rip the rest of my clothes from the clothes horse, and grabbing my pack from the hall cupboard, jam them into it.

I rush around, picking up everything I can see – clothes, laptop, sleeping bag, toothbrush. I'm panicking, grabbing shit that I don't need and throwing it down again. I keep looking at the door, half expecting the skinhead to come staggering in, a gaping bloody hole through his torso.

When I go to open the top drawer of the dresser in my bedroom I see immediately the pile of socks sitting on top of it. I didn't leave them there. I pull open the drawer, and the thing I need the most is gone: my passport. Holding the torch in my mouth, I pull out all the drawers and throw them on the bed, but it's hopeless; I know that I put it in the top drawer the day I moved in, and haven't touched it since. Grabbing my pack, I turn to leave, and the torch beam sweeps across my bed. One of the drawers I threw onto it has slid onto the floor, dragging my pillow with it. Exposed on the bed is a big pile of euros.

Anto.

For a few seconds I stand there, disbelieving, and then I sit down on the bed to gather it up – in true Anto style it's just loose notes; hundreds and fifties, but there's a lot of them. I jam it all into the top zip pocket of my pack.

I'm about to stand and go when I glance up and through my bedroom window. There's an unobstructed view down the lane, clear to the road, and in that moment I catch a glimpse of a dark figure, just visible in the moonlight, bent double and moving along the footpath. It disappears behind a parked car, melding with the gloom.

A flood of adrenaline fires through me, and I grab my pack and go for the front door. But if there's someone out there, they'll see me as soon as I step outside. Instead, I run back to the bathroom. Unlatching the window, I open it gently, and it squeaks in protest as I push it all the way out. Here, the house is in darkness, and it's the only part that can't be seen from the lane. Dangling my pack outside, I drop it out of the window, and then climb on the sill and jump out. The gravel under my feet scrunches, and to my ears it sounds horribly loud. The shed blocks my view of the lane, and I move my head in tiny increments until I can see past it, but there are no dark figures, no movement at all. I listen but can hear nothing. I stay like that for a moment, wondering if it was a trick of the light, or my frazzled imagination, but in that instant three men enter the lane at the far end and come at a jog along it, crouched low and moving silently in single file. The person hidden behind the car suddenly emerges and joins them.

I have perhaps ten seconds, and there's only one way out. I throw my pack up onto the roof of the shed and it makes a dull thud. There's a concrete post at its corner and I put a foot on to launch myself up. It's a low roof without a gutter so it's easy enough. On my belly, I shimmy forwards across the roof until my legs are away from the edge. The iron roofing clunks beneath me, so I stop moving and just lie there as still as I can. I don't know if they've seen me. I can hear their footsteps, but they don't make any other sound.

Then they're at the front door, and suddenly I can hear whispers. My heart is pounding, and I'm holding my breath. There's a pause – a beat – and then the crash of the door slamming back against the wall tears through the night. They burst inside, yelling, and I immediately I start to move again, wriggling across the roof of the shed. I get to the far side of it, turn and swing my legs over and just as I'm about to drop down I hear a familiar voice. It's the detective, Riley. He's back outside, ranting like a madman, swearing and barking orders at his men.

I hold onto the edge of the roof and look down, trying to spot my landing before letting go. The shed backs onto the yard of a house on the road parallel to mine, but thankfully it's grass so when I land it makes no sound, and I'm away. In less than a minute I'm back at the car, and I get in as quickly as I can, flinging my pack into the back seat. I can't see anyone on the street, so I start the car and ease up the road, fighting the urge to floor it. No one follows. Reaching the main road, I turn north; I'll go to Dublin via Enniskillen so that I can stay off the main highway.

I'm five minutes out of Bundoran when a thought strikes me. Pulling over, I switch on the interior car lights, then pop open the glove box. There, sitting on top of a box of ammunition and a tobacco pouch, is my passport.

I stare at it. I should be relieved; I'm home and hosed, scot-free. I'll take the ferry to England and get a bus to Heathrow and then I'm gone, on my way back to Australia where no one can touch me. But actually I'm filled with disgust at myself, sickened to my stomach. I'm running like a coward, leaving behind a trail of destruction and tragedy all of my own making.

I think of Sinead. I have an awful vision of her scrambling, trying to get away from the men, calling out for help. I can hear them laughing at her. As I sit there in the car, my disgust grows, and then it's replaced by anger; at the skinhead and his goon mate, at the fuckwit whose head I stoved in.

My rage spreads, metastasises. It fills the hole left by my grief for Sinead, by my heartbreak, by my cowardice.

With barely a conscious thought, I find myself U-turning and speeding back to Bundoran.

It only takes a minute to find the right house. I pull up, get out of the car and walk as quietly as I can down the driveway. When I reach the wheelie bin I flip the lid back and gently lie the whole thing down on its side. Then, slowly, I lift the base until I hear the contents start to slide. Some aluminium cans tinkle out, but it's only when I hear the soft clunk of the gun on the concrete that I lower the bin to the ground again.

The pistol feels like a lead weight in my hand as I walk back to the car.

Chapter 27

There isn't a soul on the roads, and nothing moves in the lane around the back of the Merchant's headquarters. A smudge of grey light is establishing itself in the east, battling against an ugly bank of cloud that's holding down the night. It's freezing cold, and a strong wind sucks plastic bags and leaves into a vortex by a garage that backs onto the lane.

I can see the pole with the camera on top from where I'm standing – tucked into a recess where a gate opens into the back of the property that neighbours the Merchant's. The camera points directly over the top of the gate.

There's a salt taste in my mouth, and I realise that the wound where the skinhead hit me with his gun must have reopened because I'm nervously chewing on my lips. I spit out the blood, and take five deep, hard breaths, then walk to the gate and stand, staring up at the camera. My heart beats like a drum.

For a full minute, nothing happens, and I think I'm going to have to find some way of getting over the wall. But then I hear footsteps and the screech of the bolt drawing back. The door opens a crack, and the muzzle of a pistol noses through it. I hold up my hands, and have to fight the urge to turn and run.

The door opens, and the tall skinny lad that met Anto and me last time – Johnny – stands there. He's dishevelled, and his eyes are bloodshot, his pupils huge in the gloom.

He looks at me in disbelief, as though he's seeing a ghost.

"Fuck me," he says. "Get in here."

I step inside and Johnny bolts the door behind me. I keep my hands up.

He orders me to turn around, slowly. I feel him lift my sweatshirt and check for weapons, and then he pats down the rest of me. I turn back to face him.

"I need to see the Merchant – now," I say. "Anto's leaving the country."

I can see the fear and indecision in Johnny's face. He keeps the gun on me, and stands there, thinking.

"His plane leaves in three hours," I say.

That spurs Johnny into action. He pushes me up the steps to the open door and we walk down the hallway. The lights are off, and I have to run my hands along the walls. When we reach the end, Johnny pulls out his phone for its torch, and tells me to lie on the floor, face-down. He unlocks the door that opens into the lounge, and tells me crawl through it and then lie flat again on the stinking carpet. The only light in the room is from the TV – it's still on, the sound muted – and I'm facing it directly. An infomercial is playing; a woman, botoxed to the eyeballs, is applying makeup.

"Darren!" yells Johnny.

He has to repeat himself twice before a door swings open and the Merchant comes out. He's wearing only a towel, wrapped around his waist. The tattoos on his arms go up to his shoulders and spread across his torso, dense and black. He's like an anatomy model in a school science lab; sinew and ligaments and muscles like ropes ripple beneath his skin.

"The fuck?" he begins, but tails off. He looks hard at Johnny. "Where are the boys?"

"No fucking idea," says Johnny. "This arsehole says Anto's going to leave the country."

"Call them," orders the Merchant.

I don't say a word. I don't even look up. The Merchant is silent for a moment. He paces the room, thinking. Johnny makes the call.

We stand there in the silence, until Johnny shakes his head.

"No answer," he says.

The Merchant scowls.

"Get up," he says.

I stand and face him. I try to control my breathing.

"Anto sold your gear, but I'm guessing you already know that," I say. My voice threatens to crack. "I can take you to him."

The Merchant's eyes narrow. The muscles in his jaw bulge and flex, and it sets off a vein throbbing in his temple. He stares at me for a long time.

"You haven't got much time," I say.

Johnny speaks: "Says Anto's catching a plane in three hours."

"That right?" the Merchant says to me. "Where's he going?"

"No idea," I reply. "He didn't say."

The Merchant scowls.

"And why the fuck would you show me where he is?" he says.

"Because he screwed me over too. And I know that if you don't get your money you'll never stop looking for me."

The Merchant says nothing. He turns and walks back through the door, and in less than a minute he's back out, dressed. He's pushing bullets into a revolver and he snaps the barrel back into place.

He walks straight over to me, and puts the gun to my forehead. My stomach twists in knots.

"Where?"

"I'm not telling you," I reply. "I'll show you, but you have to let me go."

The Merchant bares his teeth.

"How about I shoot you in the head right now?"

I stare back at him.

"Then you'll never get your money," I say.

"Got the keys?" the Merchant asks Johnny, and Johnny taps his pocket.

"Let's go," says the Merchant.

Johnny starts down the hallway first. The Merchant jabs me in the back with his gun, indicating to follow him. Johnny holds open the steel door and shuts it behind us.

Outside, the wind has risen further; it whines through the powerlines over the lane, and somewhere down the street a gate slams over and over. We turn right, and walk quickly. Both of them tuck their pistols under their arms. The Merchant walks behind me.

"You know what's going to happen if I find out you're lying, right?" he says. "You wouldn't be that fucking stupid, would you now?" His words chill me to the bone, but I'm also filled with anger – a white-hot hatred.

Near the end of the lane sits a white BMW with blacked-out windows and lowered suspension. I know straightaway it's the Merchant's.

He wants to drive, and Johnny sits directly behind me in the back seat.

The Merchant starts the engine.

"Where?" he barks.

"Finglas. Ballymore Towers," I reply, and the Merchant floors it; the BMW fishtails out of the lane, its tyres hissing on the street.

There's zero traffic, and we're there in under ten minutes. On the way I tell him that there are two lads in the flat with Anto, and all three of them have guns. I spin them a yarn; that one of them's a bare-knuckle boxer – a real animal.

The Merchant asks me about the layout of the flat and I struggle to remember; all I can see is the look on the faces of Anto's mates back in the lounge. I can't recall anything else, so I make it up; I say the two bedrooms are the first two doors on the left as you go down the hallway.

I tell the Merchant to park across the road, and point out the fifth door along on the fourth floor to The Merchant and Johnny.

"I'll go," says Johnny, but the Merchant tells him we're all going.

Johnny jabs me hard in the back of my neck with the barrel of his revolver, and I round on him and tell him to fuck off as I get out of the car. He gets out too, and squares up to me, but the Merchant's having none of it, hissing at Johnny to settle down.

I'm struggling to stay in control, to think clearly.

We go up the stairwell to the fourth floor, and I give silent thanks that there's no one in it. Emerging onto the balcony, Johnny goes first, with me in the middle and the Merchant following behind. None of the lights along the balcony work any more, and the streetlamps cast a ghostly white glow along the passage. Johnny's nervous as fuck, looking all around him as he goes.

When we reach the door to the flat, the Merchant pushes past me and we all stand silently outside for a few seconds.

"It's definitely this one?" asks the Merchant, and I nod back. He and Johnny psyche themselves up to bust open the door, and in that moment I'm forgotten. When Johnny slams the heel of his shoe into the door, I look up. It's dark, but I can see that the gun I duct-taped to the underside of the balcony above is still there.

Johnny and the Merchant rush into the hallway of the flat and through the door I can see that there are no rooms on the left-hand side.

Time comes to a halt. As I reach up for the gun, it feels as though the very air has thickened. It seems to take an age to close my fingers around it, and I feel weak and slow as the duct tape releases its grip.

But I get it into my hand, and looking back into the flat, I can see that Johnny's already at the end of the hallway. But the Merchant hesitates, turns back. He senses that something's wrong.

The Merchant's eyes go like saucers when he spots the gun. I'm pointing it directly at him, but my hand is shaking badly. He doesn't say a word; just stares straight at me. He holds his own gun down by his side.

Five seconds go by, and Johnny's voice comes down the hallway.

"There's no one here," he shouts.

The Merchant is lightning-quick as he drops to one knee and brings up his gun.

I'm barely conscious of squeezing the trigger. The revolver leaps in my hand and roars in the dark, and it seems like an optical illusion because the Merchant is instantly on his back; his hands clutched to his chest.

I stand there, shocked and unable to move, and Johnny reappears back in the hallway and stops when he sees the Merchant on the ground. For a moment he's confused; and when he looks at me I shout at him not to move. I have the revolver pointed at his head.

A yellow shaft of streetlight illuminates the Merchant's hand as it drops away from his chest, a crimson smear across the palm. I hear him take his last few breaths; weak, wet rattles, and then there's silence.

I look up at Johnny. His eyes are wild, haunted. He looks like a deer in the headlights.

"Do I have to shoot you, too?" I say to him, and he shakes his head. I step back and he goes past me, breaking into a run along the balcony.

Epilogue

The barman at Bobby's Surf Camp in G-Land remembers me. "My friend," he beams, "you come back. You want Bintang?"

I want Bintang. I've been travelling for two days solid, without any sleep. I caught the ferry from Rosslare to Fishguard in Wales, and I thought my heart was going to explode as I waited in the queue to board, expecting the detective and his men to step out at any moment. It was only on the bus to Heathrow that I started to breathe again. I caught the first Garuda Airways flight to Bali and booked a room here as soon as I arrived at the airport.

Each time I began to drift off on the plane, a flickering procession of images, like a silent movie, marched before my eyes. It was the small details that came to me; Sinead's hand, curled like an autumn leaf; the way her hair suddenly looked like a wig on a mannequin, her lifeless body suddenly not like a person any more, but an imitation, a waxwork.

I'd jerk back awake, the guilt would crash back in, and I'd order another drink.

I ask the barman how many people are staying at the camp, and he tells me all the camps are full to brimming.

"Big waves tomorrow," he says, nodding and grinning.

"Very big," I agree. I saw a weather map on the TV at the airport. The time lapse showed a purple blob spreading across the charts like a cancer; a four-metre swell created by a storm south of Indonesia is heading this way. The wind is swirling; forecast to come from three different directions over the course of the day.

I don't have a board; I left mine in the shed in Bundoran. Surfing is the last thing on my mind, anyway.

I drink six Bintangs and because I'm so shot they make my head spin. I order a mee goreng and scoff it down and my throat burns with the chilli and forty-eight hours of air conditioning. The bar is getting busy, and the noise of the chatter sounds like a roar in my head, so I leave and go to my room and crawl under the mozzie net and just lie there on the bed, fully clothed.

The hum of the jungle comes in through the windows, meeting the buzz in my brain. Thoughts cycle endlessly, ruthlessly, through my mind. I want to bash my head against the wall, to knock myself out, to find oblivion somehow.

I get up and go back to the bar and manage to convince the guy to sell me a bottle of bourbon and five small bottles of Coke and I take them back to my room and sit there, pouring them strong and drinking fast. The Coke goes warm after the first two, but I don't go back to the bar for ice. I just sit there, skulling them back, until all the Coke is gone and half of the bourbon. Now I'm well pissed, and I lie back on the bed and finally, mercifully, I'm overtaken, bulldozed into a dreamless sleep.

It's hot, and the sun is well up in the sky, when I wake the next day. I'm sweating like a dog. A brutal headache is underway, and it's all I can do to grovel over to my pack for Panadol and pull off my clothes. I fall asleep again, and when I next wake and check my phone it's past midday.

But I feel better; my headache's gone, although the torment in my mind remains. I pull on some board shorts, get two bottles of water from the bar and take a walk down to the beach.

Not even the thick jungle can hold back the sound of the ocean; an insistent, sibilant hiss filters through the foliage. Emerging from the trees, a saltwater haze fills the air. The surf is huge, grinding and pounding along the reef in a tumultuous procession. Huge pistons of water jet into the air as the waves collapse into whitewater, which churns and slides across the spume-streaked sea like an avalanche.

I'm mesmerised; awed by its power. It's also strangely calming; somehow the fury of the ocean eclipses what's going on in my head, neutralising and suppressing it, and I sit on the sand for a while, just watching it, absorbing its therapeutic energy. I lie back, close my eyes, and think of Sinead – this time not the dead Sinead, but my Sinead; beautiful and warm and kind and funny. Tears squeeze from my eyes and I feel them running down my temples, but I don't brush them away. I stay like that for a long time, grieving, my heart broken, the guilt tearing me asunder.

When I finally open my eyes I see a troupe of monkeys in the trees above me. They watch silently as I get up and walk back through the trees towards Bobby's.

Back in the bar, there's hardly anyone around. An Aussie girl tells me most of them have gone to Tiger Tracks or 20/20s to surf. I order a tuna salad and I have to force it down. I spend the afternoon in the bar, drinking mango smoothies and looking at old surf mags. I can't concentrate on any of the stories.

The barman from last night comes on for his shift, and stops as he collects my glass.

"You surf today, no?"

"I don't have a board," I reply.

"Plenty boards here – outside, in the rack," he says. "You're welcome. Bobby's boards all have scribble – a mark – on the nose."

He goes back to the bar.

Some of the surfers have returned and begun to filter into the lounge. When I ask they tell me the surf has organised itself a bit, but it's still huge.

"It'll be all-time tomorrow," an American guy says.

It's almost five o'clock when I finally get up off the couch. I'm fidgety, apprehensive. My guilt feeds my anxiety, building from a simmering unease to something approaching a panic attack. I've come to a decision: tomorrow I'll go around the rest of the surf camps to look for Anto. I need to talk to him; to tell him what he's done.

I run down to the beach, hoping for reprieve, for the wild ocean to work its magic again. But this time there's no relief. I take to throwing rocks at trees until my shoulder hurts, and then I sit and stare out to sea.

It's when I turn and look as far up the point as I can that I catch a fleeting glimpse of a dark figure going over the crest of an enormous wave. I'm not sure if I imagined it, because for a long time I don't see it again, and the sun is dropping and the glare is powerful. But then I see it again, and this time I can tell that it's a surfer out there, way up at Kongs, alone in the maelstrom.

I'm possessed by a dangerous indifference to my own welfare; I no longer care what happens to me.

I run back through the jungle to Bobby's, and find the surfboard rack. Sure enough, there's half a dozen boards with a marker-pen scribble on the nose. They're old and yellowing, abandoned by visitors to the surf camp over the years. I pick the longest one. There's a wax comb on a piece of wire, and I scrape it over the hardened, sandy wax, and then tuck the board under my arm. There's a leggie on it, but I know it won't withstand what's going on out there for very long. I don't care any more.

Back at the beach, I jog up to the keyhole. I don't even look at the waves. It's only when I'm attaching the leggie that I realise a decent offshore wind has sprung up.

I paddle out and almost immediately get mown down by a wall of whitewater, and then another, and my heart's in my mouth as I approach the impact line of the waves, but I get a lucky lull and then I'm through into the channel. I've been pushed well down in the bay and I paddle for a long time. I can't see the other surfer, and I begin to wonder if he's gone in, or even if I imagined seeing him. I'm in survival mode, and mercifully it banishes all thought.

The offshore works its magic quickly. In the ten minutes it takes me to get halfway to the top of Moneytrees, the swells have been brushed clean, textured by a stipple of goosebumps. The waves start to align, to adhere to the reef. A fifteen-foot bomb comes out of nowhere, but I'm deep enough in the channel to get around it, so I stop paddling to watch it go by. Its huge wall is emerald; its giant plume a flamboyant golden crest in the setting sun. Topping it, I see that it's the first of a set; its clone thunders towards me. The noise as it breaks is incredible, and it scares the shit out of me, but feeling fear and nothing else is a blessed relief for now. I stare into the depths of its huge barrel as I go over it.

The last wave of the set is the biggest, and on it Anto rides out of the sun. He's a hundred metres away and I can see little more than his silhouette, but I know immediately that it's him; his stance – tall, defiant, triumphant – gives him away. He draws out a long bottom turn, and then halfway up the face he jams hard under the lip. He's precocious, disrespectful of the wave's size and immense power. The wave roars up behind him. He doesn't panic, doesn't pump. He's overtaken, engulfed by it. He's in the eye of the hurricane. He rises up the face, and it rockets him forward. He flies through the belly of the wave, untouched, untouchable, a matador toying with a bull.

He's twenty metres away, still locked in, supersonic, when his eyes finally flick to me.

Anto opens his mouth wide, and howls like a wolf.

Author's note:

I hope you enjoyed reading LINES as much as I enjoyed writing it.

I don't have the big budgets of traditional publishers, but I do have something much, much better – people who talk about my books, and reader reviews.

I'd be delighted if you'd take five minutes to review/rate the book on **amazon.com** or **goodreads.com** (or both). It can be as short or as long as you like. It makes all the difference to indie authors like myself. Thanks in advance!

James

Also, by the author

MINE

Twenty-six-year-old Jimmy Brennan's life has taken a turn for the worse, and he's desperate to numb the pain. When his mother dies and his girlfriend betrays him, it's the final straw: he leaves Australia, bound for Bali.

But Jimmy's demons chase him. Sickened by the filth and the rapacious tourists swarming the Indonesian holiday island, Jimmy escapes north up the archipelago, driven by a desire for solitude and possessed by a reckless, self-destructive urge.

When he's offered the opportunity to visit the forbidden island of North Sentinel, home of a forgotten tribe which has violently rejected outside contact for centuries, Jimmy takes it.

He finds paradise, but it's a discovery that will have deadly consequences.

"Fast-paced and utterly immersive, with surfing passages that will have your heart leaping into your throat and your muscles twitching to do the same – a must-read for surfers and non-surfers alike. This is 'Breath' meets 'The Beach', but also a unique tale in its own right that will stay with the reader long after they read the last page."
Eileen Merriman, best-selling author of Violet Black and The Silence of Snow

"Exceptional. Like a good hold down it wouldn't let me up"
Ray Bisschop, publishing director, Surfing Life

"A life or death, immersive ride"
Louise Ward, Wardini Books

"Electrifying!"
Justin Brown, author of Bowling Through India and UK on a G-String

"Ripped through it in a weekend"
Luke Kennedy, editor, Tracks mag

Books by James Russell
for younger readers

The Dragon Hunters, The Dragon Tamers and The Dragon Riders
are best-selling picture books for children aged 3-7,
and published in a dozen countries.

The five books in The Dragon Defenders series of junior novels
are for children aged 8-12. They are also best sellers, with over
50,000 copies sold.

Find out more at www.dragonbrothersbooks.com